HER DEFIANT WARRIOR

OMEGA SKY
BOOK 5

CAITLYN O'LEARY

© Copyright 2023 Caitlyn O'Leary
All rights reserved.
All cover art and logo © Copyright 2023
By Passionately Kind Publishing Inc.
Cover by Lori Jackson Design
Edited by Sally Keller
Content Edited by Trenda Lundin
Technical Editor, Lauren Johnson
Cover Photo by Wander Aguiar Photography

All rights reserved. No part of this book may be reproduced in any form or by any electronic or mechanical means, including information storage and retrieval systems—except in the case of brief quotations embodied in critical articles or reviews—without permission in writing from the author.

This book is a work of fiction. The names, characters, and places portrayed in this book are entirely products of the author's imagination or used fictitiously. Any resemblance to actual events, locales or persons, living or dead, is entirely coincidental and not intended by the author.

The unauthorized reproduction or distribution of this copyrighted work is illegal. Criminal copyright infringement, including infringement without monetary gain, is investigated by the FBI and is punishable by up to five years in federal prison and a fine of $250,000.

If you find any eBooks being sold or shared illegally, please contact the author at Caitlyn@CaitlynOLeary.com.

To every single mom out there. You women are amazing. I wish you all of the love you deserve, and may you all find your Jase.

SYNOPSIS

Will winning her heart be enough to overcome her fear of losing him?

What starts out as a forced blind date might just be the best thing that ever happened to Jase and Bonnie.

Navy SEAL Jase Drakos is used to pulse-pounding missions that often mean the difference between life and death. He balances his job with his large and loving family and the team of men who have turned into brothers. But Jase has come to realize that something is missing in his world. So maybe it's time to come to terms with the fact that he's going to end up going through life without a woman by his side and a family of his own.

Single mother Bonnie Larkin doesn't know if she is a chambermaid, chef, or chauffeur. Raising seven-year-old twins has her hopping, especially since they are precocious and love trying out their next grand adventure. She is mostly fine with their antics because she knows their shenanigans break up the monotony of her otherwise lackluster life. After all, her one big adventure left her pregnant and alone before she was eighteen, so monotony was good, wasn't it?

Can Jase tempt Bonnie into a life filled with love, laughter, and color, even though loving him means learning to live with his job's risks? And what happens when Bonnie gets to see the terror of his job, up close and personal?

This is an action, adventure, romantic, stand-alone novel.

PROLOGUE

Fourteen-year-old Jase Drakos watched his mother's eyes squint as the little man in charge of the orphanage thanked her again for attending their celebration along with the city delegation. Somehow the little town had scrounged up twenty people who thought highly of themselves, three reporters and that one guy with a video camera...and Jase's mom.

"Your support means the world to us, Mrs. Drakos. Our mayor said you were a big supporter for the orphanages in Peru. You can see how happy and clean our children are. We do good work here." The four hairs on his head dripped with sweat.

Jase elbowed his Peruvian brother Renzo in the ribs when the younger boy snorted with laughter.

"Shut it," Jase whispered. Renzo looked back at Jase and nodded. They both knew it was important not to call attention to themselves. Luckily, their mom didn't look their way.

"I'm sure these reporters here will provide the

publicity you need to get plenty of donations, Mr. Garcia." Their mother smiled. Jase recognized it. It was her fake smile. He remembered it when Elani had cooked charcoal cookies and his mom had choked two of them down and said how good they were.

"Ah, but you were able to get many rich Americans to donate to orphanages in Peru. Perhaps you can work your magic here in Brazil as well."

At fourteen, Jase knew when someone was pulling a fast one, and this guy was a weasel. He had totally put their mom on the spot.

"Come on, let's go." Jase jerked his head at Renzo and their other brother Malik.

They moved away from the crowd and made their way back into the now empty classroom where the weasel had made the orphans perform. Renzo and Malik turned to look at Jase.

"What's the plan?" Renzo asked.

"He doesn't have one," Malik snorted. "He never has one. And the fool expects us to follow him."

"And you do. So, who's the fool?" Jase smirked back at his youngest brother.

"Okay, Mr. No Plan, why are we back here? What are we looking for?" Malik goaded.

"Something doesn't smell right. Mom could tell too. She wasn't buying what that guy was selling. Did you believe him?" Jase asked Malik, who shook his head. "Did you?" he said, turning his attention to Renzo.

"Fuck no," Renzo responded.

Jase snickered. Listening to Renzo say fuck with his Spanish accent always cracked him up.

"So, what do you think is wrong?" Jase asked Renzo.

"Aren't you going to ask me?" Malik asked.

"Nope. Renzo's the only one of us who actually lived in an orphanage. You lived with your parents 'til they died. Then Mom and Dad adopted you. Mom and Dad adopted me when I was a baby, so that means we don't know what it's like in an orphanage. Renzo does. This place gives me the heebie jeebies. And if *I* think something stinks, and Mom's kind of worried, then I really want to know what Renzo thinks."

"Makes sense." Malik nodded. "But what could they be doing? You saw all the kids; they were all laughing and singing and fingerpainting. Do you think that butthole is going to steal the donations?"

"They might steal the donations," Renzo answered. "But you better not believe all the kids are happy. They pulled that shit at my orphanage in Peru. Then they hid the sick, injured, and uncontrollable kids in the basement."

"They did?" Malik asked. His eyes were wide. "Why would they do that?"

"They didn't want visitors to see them, right?" Jase asked Renzo.

"I wish it was only those times," Renzo said harshly. "One kid who came at the same time I did kept crying all the time. He was just a couple of years younger than me. His mom had been killed right in front of him. I think they did things to her too. He saw it all. He screamed in his sleep almost every night. He couldn't help it."

Renzo stopped talking. He dug his toe into the cracked cement floor.

"What happened to him?" Malik asked.

"I tried to make him stop crying. He was just a little kid, ya' know? He slept in the bunk beneath mine, so I would creep down and wake him up when he was having a nightmare so the warden wouldn't punish him."

"I don't get it. Why would they punish him? He was just having a nightmare, right?" Malik questioned Renzo again.

Renzo sighed. "Right," he said. "Twice he wet his bed. When he did, the warden lady would rub his nose in the pee sheets. Then he threw up, and she beat his butt with her stick. The third time that happened, they took him away."

"What do you mean, they took him away?" Jase asked. "They took him away where?"

"To one of the punishment rooms in the basement. There were three of them. I saw them when I escaped. I tried to take Edmundo with us, but he could barely walk or talk. He'd been down in the basement too long. I wanted to kill the wardens. Almost all of them were devils."

"You really think it's the same here?" Jase asked solemnly.

Renzo nodded. "All the children were too happy. Too pretty. Too healthy. I'm positive the wardens here are lying."

"You mean the teachers?" Malik asked.

"Don't believe it," Renzo said. "There might be one

or two who are nice, but some of them, especially that weasel-man, are evil."

Jase shuddered. He was scared. Not of any warden. His mom would save them. He was scared of what they would find. He was terrified that there were little kids like Edmundo behind the back door. He knew something was wrong, but it couldn't be that bad, could it?

"You're making this up." Malik frowned at Renzo. Jase could tell that Malik was only arguing because he didn't want the things Renzo was saying to be true.

"You'll see," Renzo said with quiet authority. "Now we need to be quiet. We need to find the other kids."

Jase nodded at Renzo. In the corner of the room, there was a door painted the same color as the walls. Jase had remembered how mad the weasel man had gotten when one of the teachers had opened it. He'd yelled at her in Portuguese to not be so stupid. He nodded at Renzo. That was their target. They went over and opened it. It led to a hallway painted puke green.

It smelled like piss.

"Eww. Somebody needs their diaper changed," Malik said as he made a face.

Renzo shook his head. "Trust me, it's going to get a lot worse."

The hall was long. They carefully tried every door along the way. In every room they could get into, all they found were thin mattresses on the floors, some with blankets and pillows, some without. Two doors were locked.

"That's where the wardens live," Renzo said in a serious tone.

"How can you know that?" Jase asked.

"They always lock their doors. They don't want anyone to see how good they've got it. And they don't want anyone to see their punishment sticks and things. In my orphanage, they even had those electric things that they used on the bulls." Renzo shuddered.

Jase tried to make sense of what Renzo was saying. Finally, it sank in. "Cattle prods?"

"I think so. They go zap on the cows and make them hurt and make them move. They really hurt us kids. They only used it on me once. It was enough."

Fuck. No wonder Renzo ran away from the orphanage and went to go live on the streets of Peru.

They continued down the hallway. As they got close to the end, they all heard crying and screaming.

Oh God, it's going to be as bad as Renzo said.

"It really, really stinks," Malik said.

"Shut your cake hole," Renzo whisper hissed.

Jase tried to laugh at his Peruvian brother for saying cake instead of pie, but he was too sick and scared about what they were going to find. At the end of the hall, they had to turn right, which led to double doors. They had small windows at the top. Jase and Malik were the tallest. They both looked through the small windows.

"Oh my God," Malik said as he crossed himself.

"What?" Renzo demanded to know.

Jase turned to Renzo. "It's okay, we can go in. There's no grown-up in there."

"Yeah, because they've locked the kids up in cages," Malik practically yelled.

"Be quiet," Renzo hissed at Malik.

"Shut up!" Jase said at the same time. "Let's go. We gotta help them."

"We can't," Renzo said.

"Yes, we can," Jase said emphatically. "There is no way that Mom will put up with this shit. She'll report them."

He pushed open the door and went in. The wave of sound almost knocked him on his butt. There was no rhyme or reason to how the orphans were divided up into the five large cages. Each cage had a thick chain and padlock locking the doors shut. Big kids and little kids were put together, boys and girls were locked in together. There were blankets strewn about the cement floor, but no pillows. He saw a crib in each cage, but only the littlest of babies were crammed in them. The smell of urine and shit was almost as bad as the crying, pleading, and screaming.

"We've gotta let 'em out. Look for a key," Jase demanded as he turned to his younger brothers.

"No," Renzo said flatly. "It'll cause chaos. We need to show Mom and that guy with the camera. Then they'll see what's really going on."

Jase looked over at the cage furthest from the double doors. Two older kids were clutching at the bars. One of them was pounding his head against a bar, and there was blood dripping from his forehead.

"Okay, then we've got to get them, quick. That kid is

bleeding!" Jase said as he ran toward the cage with the wounded child.

"I found them," Malik said.

"What?" Renzo and Jase said as they saw Malik jogging after them. The keys were hanging from the back wall. All three of them stopped in front of the cage with the bloody boy.

"Jase, you go get Mom and the reporters. She'll listen to you. I'll go in and try to calm them down," Renzo said.

Jase nodded, but then he saw something out of the corner of his eye, in the next cage over.

"Stop that," Jase yelled in Portuguese.

A boy, maybe five years old, swung a naked baby by her arm. She wasn't making a sound. Then he dropped her and laughed. The baby, no toddler, tried to lift up on her hands and knees, but she fell flat, her injured arm unable to hold her up. The cruel boy shoved at her with his foot. Another kid, a girl this time, grabbed at the baby's curly black hair.

"*Sua merda*," she shouted in her face, then spit in the baby's face.

"Leave her alone!" Jase yelled again in Portuguese as he shook the cage door.

An older girl from the cage next door chimed in. "Little *puta*. Her mama is nothing but a rotten cop's whore. Kick her again."

"Just wait until I get my knife back," another boy from two cages over said. "I'll carve my initials on her forehead. Then she won't be so pretty."

What the shit?

Jase spun around and looked at Malik. "Open the cage!"

Malik fumbled. The first key didn't work and it took Jase everything he had not to grab them from his brother. Finally, Malik found the right key and Jase pulled the chain away and yanked open the steel door to get inside the cage.

The first little boy laughed and crouched down in front of the toddler. "One day your pai will see his ugly daughter if he doesn't die in prison first. What will the big bad policeman think of his princess then? Your *mãe* was nothing but a whore and your *pai* was a butcher."

Now the baby girl was scrambling away from the two bullies. She was trying to cover herself with one of the few ratty blankets in the cage. Jase saw red when he saw the little boy pull back his leg, and he could see the little shit was going to kick her again.

Jase grabbed up the girl just in time.

Please Jesus, say I didn't hurt her more.

As the boy kicked air, he ended up falling on his ass. Jase wanted to kick him, but the little girl was his top priority.

"Get Mom," he yelled to Malik. Jase stomped out of the cage, cuddling the girl to his chest. "Close it up," he barked to Renzo.

His brother was already on it.

Jase strode to the farthest corner of the room and slid down the wall, shutting out everything but the little girl in his arms. He moved the blanket away from her face and body, carefully using the blanket to wipe the spit off her forehead. He wanted to get an idea of how badly she was injured.

Her face was gaunt, her cheekbones were high and sharp. She wasn't crying; instead she was looking up at him with no expression at all. It was as if she was someplace else. Jase looked down and saw an enormous bruise on her side where she had been kicked. There were a lot of little bruises on her arms and legs. When he looked closely, it looked like she had been pinched by tiny fingers.

"What did they do to you, Angel?"

Her arm didn't look broken, or even out of its socket, which was a minor miracle. But Jase could see the dark bruising along the fair skin of her wrist.

"It's going to be all right," Jase crooned in Portuguese. "You're safe now."

He held her on his lap, rocking her between his chest and his knees so that he could watch her face. She never took her eyes off him. She was probably waiting for the next blow. Judging from how old the bruising from the pinches was, and just how emaciated she looked, she had been neglected and abused for a very long time. It would take forever for her to trust anyone, let alone a Latino-looking kid who looked like an older version of the kid who had been about to kick her.

Jase slowly reached out and cupped the side of her head, and started humming the one song he could remember his mom singing to him when he was a baby. Then he remembered her singing it to Malik and the other kids as they came along. Jase began singing the words, and the little angel lifted her uninjured hand up to his lips.

"When I'm worried and I can't sleep

I count my blessings, instead of sheep

And I fall asleep—"

"What is going on?" his mother shouted above the noise.

Jase felt a flash of relief, but continued to sing to the little girl and feeling his heart lurch when one lone tear dripped down her cheek.

He continued to sing, even though his voice trembled.

"If you're worried and you can't sleep

Just count your blessings, instead of sheep

And you'll fall—"

"Stop! Stop! Stop! You can't go in there." It was the bald weasel yelling in Portuguese.

Jase looked up and over. He saw his mother barreling through the double doors. She was livid.

"My God! What have you done? Jase! Renzo! Where are you?"

Jase tuned her out. All that mattered was the little girl in his arms.

With his thumb, he brushed away the little girl's tear. She was getting blurry, and he couldn't understand why, until he saw a drop of water hit her chin. That was when he realized he was crying.

He tried to sing again, but he couldn't, his voice was too hoarse. He began humming the song.

"Jase?"

"Jase?"

He felt a soft touch on his shoulder and turned for just a moment to see Renzo at his side.

"Go away," he mumbled.

Renzo didn't. "We need to go talk to Mom."

"I can't. I can't leave her." He went back to humming.

Once again, the little angel reached up and touched his mouth. It was as if she was trying to feel his voice as well as hear it.

"Seriously, Bro."

Jase didn't even turn his head or acknowledge Renzo in any way. He continued to concentrate on the toddler in his arms.

Then he saw his brother's finger stroke down Angel's cheek. She jerked, then looked over at Renzo. It took almost a minute for her to settle. It was as if she knew he was one of the good guys.

"She's beautiful," Renzo said.

"They were torturing her. Little kids were beating and torturing her." Jase's voice broke. "How could they be doing that? I don't understand." He finally turned to look at Renzo.

"This place turns everyone into animals," Renzo said.

"They're evil." Jace ground out.

"The adults are evil. The kids didn't start out evil. The adults made them that way."

Jase didn't believe him. All he cared about was his angel. He had to protect her. There was no way he was leaving her.

"Look at this."

Renzo stared for long moments at the roadmap of abuse on her tiny, gaunt body. "Fuck. Maybe they are evil," he breathed out.

Renzo held out his finger, and the little girl took another long look at him.

He smiled at her, but she just had that solemn expression on her face.

"She's so thin," Renzo said. "She has to be hungry. You're hungry, aren't you, Little Angel?" he asked in Spanish.

Jase smiled. He wasn't surprised in the least that Renzo was also calling her Angel.

"Jase!" It was his mom calling.

"Here, you take her," Jase said softly as he gently transferred the girl to Renzo.

As he began walking away, he heard Renzo start humming. It was a different song, but it, too, sounded like a lullaby.

He stopped and stared when he saw that there were two men and three women who were all dressed in the light-blue teacher uniforms, surrounded by most of the spectators who had come with his mom to visit the orphanage. One of the lady teachers had two women holding her as she yelled at them. She was shouting curse words at everyone. Over and over again she screamed the children couldn't be let out of the cages. She kept saying they were filth and animals and retards.

Renzo was right; they were evil devils.

"Jase!"

He turned and saw his mother. He jogged up to

where she was towering over the little weasel of a director. The guy with the camera was filming everything.

As soon as she spotted him, he could see just how distressed she was.

"Where have you been? I've been calling for you." She reached out and put her arm around his shoulders, pulling him close.

"I'm sorry, Mom," and he meant it. "I didn't mean to worry you."

"This is awful," she whispered into the side of his head. "So awful." He heard the tremor in her voice. Then she sucked in a deep breath and turned to face him.

"Jace. I need you, Son. It's important."

"Anything." Always. He would always do anything for his mother.

She pointed at the crowd around the teachers. "Some of those people are going to go into town and contact the police. Nita is going to take you to the job site, and I want you to get your dad. I want you to bring him here. Got it?"

Now that she had a plan, and she was getting dad, she wasn't worried anymore. Now she was *mad*. Jase didn't think he'd ever seen her so mad.

"Mom, I need you to come see something first, okay?"

She reached out and cupped his cheek. She'd done that all of his life. It didn't matter that now he was inches taller than her. "I really need you to hurry, Honey," she said.

"This is important, Mom."

She winced, then nodded. "Okay, show me."

He grasped her hand and ushered her over to the corner where Renzo was holding Angel.

"She's just a little girl. Almost a baby, Mom." Jase heard his voice break. He crouched down beside Renzo. He couldn't help himself. He needed to look into her eyes. Make sure that she knew he hadn't left her.

When he held out his finger, she grasped it.

Renzo continued humming.

Jase was so busy looking at Angel's face he was startled when his mom brushed back a lock of the child's hair off her forehead. Angel pulled away from her. She grabbed at Jase with her other hand, too.

Fuck. Had that evil teacher hurt her?

He looked up at his mom, who was now kneeling on the other side of Renzo. "How bad off is she?" his mom asked.

"I saw a little boy and then a littler girl hurting her before I could stop them. The girl called her a piece of shit and spit on her," Jase quietly told his mother. "They said something about her dad being a bad cop who was in jail and her mom was a...wasn't a good mom." He didn't know how to say what they'd said.

Renzo dragged back a bit of the girl's blanket so that his mom could see the little girl's bruised side.

Jase gently stroked a finger over the baby's swelling wrist. "Mom, he was swinging her around."

Sharon closed her eyes for a moment. "Sweet mother of God."

"We can't leave her here, Mom," Renzo said.

"How is he?" Malik asked as he bent over Jase's shoulder.

"She," Jase corrected.

"How is she?" Malik asked again.

"You should hold her," Renzo said to Jase.

He nodded. The little girl was holding onto him with both of her hands. The two boys awkwardly transferred her, and she gave a little chirp of pain.

"You're hurting her," Malik cried out.

"They're helping her, Honey," Sharon assured her younger son. Once again, Jase heard his mother's voice tremble.

"Can you do something?" Malik asked.

"You're not going to leave her here, are you?" Renzo asked.

"She won't leave her," Jase assured his brother. "We're adopting her."

Sharon Drakos looked at her oldest son. Jase saw tears in her eyes and his gut clenched.

She won't say no, will she?

A tear dripped down his mother's face, as she smiled the biggest smile he'd ever seen before. "Renzo? Malik? Are you adopting her too?"

"Yes!" they both said at the same time.

Two more tears fell down her cheek.

"I have never. Not ever. Loved you boys more. Of course, we're adopting her."

1

"You're kidding me, right?" Jase looked over at his brother. "Have you lost your ever-loving mind?"

Malik sighed. "You try arguing with fourteen, fifteen- and sixteen-year-old girls when their mother is on their side. You can't win."

"But look at how she's dressed," Jase said again. He looked over at his fifteen-year-old niece and couldn't believe what he was seeing. The shiny green dress Maryanne wore went midway up her thighs and only covered one shoulder. The only saving grace was that she was wearing it with flat sneakers and not a pair of hooker heels.

"There is no way that Dad would have let any of our sisters leave the house looking like that," Jase said with confidence.

"You're right, he wouldn't. That's why all our sisters said they were spending the night with their girlfriends and carried duffle bags with their dresses, make-up, and heels inside. The way I see it, Dad didn't know where they were going, what they were doing, or who they were doing it with. Remember?"

"Fuck yeah. How often were you, me, Renzo, and Bruno following them around, making sure that nobody took advantage of them? It seemed like a full-time job. Especially with Angelica."

Malik snorted in his beer.

"Yeah, she was a wild one," he agreed. "Still is, if even a quarter of what the tabloids say is true."

"It's not," Jase assured Malik. "Angelica might be on the wild side, but she's not stupid." He gave his brother a sideways look. "Don't change the subject. So, your philosophy is that you'd prefer knowing up front how they're dressed and what they're up to, instead of them doing it behind your back?"

"Absolutely," Malik nodded. "Plus, I have an ace in the hole. Jenny is daddy's little girl," he said, referring to his youngest daughter. "I can always take her out for an ice cream sundae and she'll end up spilling her guts. If there's something I wasn't privy to, then Jenny will fill me in."

Jase nodded. "I like it. Why's Farah okay with how they're dressed?" Jase asked, referring to Malik's wife.

"Same thing as me. You gotta remember, we were wild and in love back in the day. We're trying to be open and honest with the girls so they don't fall into the same situation we did."

Jase squeezed his brother's shoulder.

"You and Farah were meant to be together. Even back then, when you got her pregnant, I knew that you two were going to make it."

"Thank God Mom and Dad did too. To this day, I'm still pissed at how Farah's parents treated her."

"Yeah, but you got over it for the girls."

"Nope, never got over it. I just put on a good face. They hurt Farah too deeply, for too long for me to be over it. They're good with the girls, so I'll put up with them, but the day they pull any shit with my daughters? They won't believe the wrath that will come down upon their heads."

Jase grinned. "I wouldn't expect anything less."

"How about you? Aren't you sick of being single by now?" Malik asked.

Before he had to answer, Maryanne giggled, left her posse, and headed their way.

"Hi Dad, hi Uncle Jase." She hugged her dad, then she hugged Jase and gave him a kiss on the cheek.

"You're too pretty for words," Jase complimented his niece.

The blush that tinted her warm brown complexion only made her prettier.

"Thanks, Uncle Jase."

"So, what are you doing, looking so good tonight?"

"There's a dance after Halsey High's football game. Johnny asked me to go to it. I'm going with a bunch of other couples."

"How many other couples? How are you getting there? When are you getting home?"

She looked over at Malik. "He's worse than you are. Actually, he's even worse than Penny's dad," she giggled. She gave Jase a sly smile. "I can't wait until you have daughters. You're going to be ancient and have no idea what's going on."

Malik snorted and gave him a smirk.

Asshole.

She reached up on her tiptoes and gave him another kiss. Then she did the same to her dad. "I'll be home by eleven," she smiled, then whirled away.

Jase looked over at his brother. "You're going to have your hands full. But wait until Lena starts dating. She's going to run circles around you."

"Nah, she posts on snapchat every half hour. I'll get a play-by-play of what's going on. If she doesn't post for over an hour, *then* I'll be worried."

Jase chuckled. "I like it."

"I'll give you step-by-step instructions on what to do when you're ancient," Malik promised.

Jase looked around his brother's big backyard. He enjoyed seeing how far he'd come from the frail, scared kid he'd been when their parents had first brought him into their home, damn near thirty years ago.

"I see that look in your eye. You're being all nostalgic."

"Yeah, it happens. Is that Renzo I see over there?" They both looked over at another Drakos brother.

"Well, hell. I invite him to every family function. I never know what country he's in. The bastard rarely replies. I can't believe he graced us with his presence."

They both watched as a tall dark-haired woman went streaking across the lawn and flung her arms around Renzo and pulled him in for a tight hug.

"Is that Angelica?" Jase asked Malik.

He nodded.

"When did our sister become a flower child? Her hair must have grown down to her ass."

"Nah. Farah clued me in. Those are extensions. I think it's for some TV show or something." They both watched as she started chattering a million miles a minute, her hands flying in all directions.

Jase chuckled. To this very day, it made his heart melt to see their Brazilian 'angel' so confident and happy.

"How long should we let that go on before we rescue him?" Malik asked.

"After he's been gone this long? I say make him suffer. At least forty-five minutes before we bring a beer over to him."

Malik laughed.

"I'm going to wander around a bit, but I'll meet you back at the grill in twenty."

Malik nodded.

Jase headed to a quiet corner that overlooked Chesapeake Bay. It was blocked off by tall potted plants so he could have a little alone time and think about what his brother had asked. He took a pull on his beer. On the other side of the potted plant, a woman began to speak.

"Hi, Bradley. Sorry I didn't call earlier. It's been a bitch of a day."

The woman's laugh was warm and musical, like she was inviting Bradley to share in a joke.

"No, nothing like that. It's just that I had to put on a dress, slather on make-up, remember how to wear heels, all while keeping the terrible twosome clean for ten minutes before we headed out the door."

There was a pause, then this time she laughed longer.

"I'll tell you why, because I lost a bet with Farah. She bet me she could talk the next customer who came into the salon into dying their hair purple. It was a good bet. She promised to watch the terrible twosome for an entire weekend if she lost."

There was a pause.

"My side? I agreed to go on a blind date with her brother-in-law, but I had to dress up and actually do my best to be flirty. You know I don't do flirty. Hell, I don't know *how* to do flirty. But that was the bet. I desperately needed a weekend off, so I took the bet."

Oh shit, does she mean me? How many times have I told Farah, no more set-ups!

The woman paused.

"Huh?" she asked softly. "Hell yeah, I stacked the deck." This time her giggle turned into a chuckle. "I knew damn good and well the next customer coming in was my bi-monthly appointment. It was Emily McCall, and she's eighty-five years old. I was going to win hands down."

Smart woman.

"Quit laughing, Bradley."

"Yes, somehow Farah talked Mrs. McCall into a pretty purple fade down to her tips. With the modern cut I finally got to do on her, she looked fifteen years younger. For that, I really owe Farah, but it's not flirt-worthy."

She sounds like she's in as much pain as I am. Interesting.

"What do I mean by that? She's been telling me about how wonderful this guy is. Kind-hearted, nice to bunny rabbits, nice to her daughters, blah, blah, blah. But here's the kicker, Farah has screwed him over one too many times, so he can't know it's a set-up. I'm supposed to flirt my way into getting him to ask me out," she whined.

She paused.

"No, I can't. What the fuck, Bradley? Nobody's going to want to ask me out, no matter how much make-up I slather on."

This pause was a lot longer.

"I get that. I know I can clean up well, but I have Amber and Lachlan with me. I'm on wrangler duty. I don't know how Farah thinks that even with heels, a dress, and make-up, some guy is going to be interested in some stylist with two kids."

She giggle-snorted.

"You're full of shit, Bradley. There's no such thing as Prince Charming or a happily ever after. I learned that the hard way. Anyway, a man who's older than thirty-five and who's never been married is either gay or a player."

"Is too!" she refuted whatever Bradley said.

"But I lost the bet, fair and square. So, I'll flirt with him in front of Farah so she can see I've tried, then I'll tell him I have two kids, and he'll run and hide. Easy, breezy."

She sighed.

"Why couldn't *you* have been straight? You would have been a perfect husband and father."

She laughed hard.

I sure would have liked to have heard what Bradley had said.

"Okay, except for the fact that you chew tobacco and you're a diehard Lakers fan. Come on man, you live in Chicago, root for the home team."

Jase had to hold in a laugh so she wouldn't know he was there.

"Okay honey, gotta go. Thanks for listening to me. Gotta make sure that Amber hasn't talked Lachlan into jumping from the roof into the pool. Then gotta go chat up some guy. Hope I remember how."

Another pause.

"Yeah, yeah, yeah. You're good for my ego. But I know the truth, and I look like a stuffed sausage in this dress. He won't even get to where he finds out about the kids. The body will turn him off before we even get to that point. Now this time, for real, gotta go."

Jase could tell she was off the phone.

She chuckled. "Well, here goes nothing."

Once again, Bonnie had to bite the inside of her cheek when she confronted her twins. Thank God they inherited more of the Larkins' mischievous nature and not the Phillips' stuffy side, otherwise she would have been bored to death.

"Lachlan, explain what happened." She frowned at her son.

"It was an accident," Amber piped up.

Bonnie narrowed her eyes and looked at her seven-year-old daughter. "I'm sorry. Did I say your name? I don't remember saying your name when I asked that question. Lachlan, did I ask Amber a question?" Bonnie hated the fact that there were two big men behind her, listening in to this conversation, but after having raised her children alone for the last seven years, she'd had to gain a thick skin. Anyway, all things considered, this was a relatively minor problem.

"No, Mom," he answered reluctantly.

Of course, he was reluctant to agree with her. Amber always came up with the best stories to get the two of them out of trouble. Lachlan was the weak link.

"So, Lachlan. Please explain how Maryanne's dog Punk got out of the garage and was in her room, along with your shoes and the remains of Mrs. Drakos' cherry pie."

"Mom, if you would just listen to me, I can explain," Amber broke in again.

"Amber, if you try to talk one more time, I am taking away your tablet time for a month. Got it?"

"Yes, Mom." Losing tablet privileges was huge. That would definitely stop her daughter from chiming in.

Bonnie heard one man cough. She knew what that meant; they were trying to cover up a laugh. They better not laugh. If they started, she just knew she'd join in. She needed to concentrate on something else. She looked down at Lachlan's feet and wondered how his cherry-stained socks could possibly have a hole in them. She'd just bought him new socks a month ago.

She looked into blue eyes that were a mirror of her own. "Explain, mister."

"I heard Punk whining in the garage, and you could tell he wasn't happy. We wanted to play with him, but we knew Mr. Drakos didn't want him at the party."

"Not *we*," Amber whispered.

"I mean I. *I* wanted to play with him," Lachlan corrected. "Anyways, *I* knew he was Maryanne's dog, so *I* thought he would be happier in her room."

"How'd you know which room belonged to Maryanne?" Bonnie asked.

Lachlan's gaze shifted over to his sister, then looked back down at his feet. "I guessed."

"Okay, you guessed. What made you guess that room, instead of one of her sister's?"

"I don't know. Maybe because." He tugged down the front of his Iron Man shirt with his cherry-stained hands. "Because."

"Because why?" Bonnie asked softly.

"Green," Amber whispered out of the side of her mouth.

"Oh," he brightened. "Because it had a green pillow on her bed like her dress?" His eyes were hopeful as he looked over at Amber.

"I need you to look at *me* when you're talking to me," Bonnie admonished.

Her boy looked up at her reluctantly.

"And the pie? How'd the pie get up there?"

"Cherry pie is my favorite. I thought he'd like it, and he did. So, I was right, right?" He hit her with that charming smile, the one with the dimple.

The little thug.

Bonnie did her best to look cross, but she could tell

it wasn't working, because he grinned bigger. "Cherry pie is your favorite too, right, Mom?"

This time, there wasn't even a cough behind her. She heard a definite choking sound.

Jackasses.

"And your shoes?"

"I shouldn't have put the pie on her bed, 'cause Punk made a mess. The pie got all over the covers, and then it fell on me and onto the carpet. I didn't want to leave footprints, so I took off my shoes. Pretty good, huh?"

"Shouldn't have left evidence behind," her daughter muttered.

"Huh?" Lachlan looked over at his sister.

"Nothing," she said as she swiftly glanced up at her mother.

"Lachlan, did you know what you were doing was wrong?"

"Uhmmm."

"Think carefully," Bonnie warned.

Bonnie stopped talking. Silence always killed her son.

"Uhmmm, not wrong, exactly? I mean, Punk was happy. That part was good, right? I mean, so if part was right, and part was wrong, then everything's okay, right?"

Malik sounded like he needed the Heimlich maneuver. He was choking so badly. She needed to get this under control. Now!

"Lachlan Kenneth Larkin, is that your final answer? And Amber Megan Larkin, you think carefully too. Did you think this was wrong?"

Bonnie started to count to sixty in her head. She watched her children squirm.

She got to forty-five.

The two of them sounded like auctioneers as they talked over one another.

"I'm sorry. I knew it was wrong. I shouldn't have done it. I just wanted to play with Punk, and I wanted to give him a treat," Lachlan whimpered.

"It wasn't all him. I wanted to play with him too, but I told him we should give him only a piece of cake."

"What are you going to do about this?" Bonnie asked in her best stern-mother voice.

"We'll clean up the mess," Amber promised.

"Clean?" Lachlan asked. He was obviously appalled.

"Yes," Bonnie answered. "Clean."

"But there's throw-up," Lachlan whined. "Punk throwed-up all over Maryanne's room."

"That's because dogs shouldn't eat pie. Let's ask Mr. Drakos if he has cleaning supplies for us to clean with, shall we?"

She turned to look at Malik and saw that she'd drawn a crowd.

Great. One of them has to be the brother that Farah wants me to meet. Well, at least this will stop that *bullshit in its tracks.*

She turned back to her hellions. Luckily, they were too absorbed at the thought of throw-up to notice Farah giggling. "Okay, you two think about how you're going to clean the mess upstairs."

She left the two of them to think, then turned to

talk to Farah and Malik. "I can't tell you how sorry I am about this." Bonnie closed her eyes for a moment. "I wish I could say this is a onetime occurrence, but this type of thing keeps happening, and it's always something new. So, once I tell them, 'You can't do that', they come up with something entirely different."

Bonnie bit her bottom lip.

"It's fine, honey," Farah assured her. "You should have seen our three girls at that age. They were hell on wheels."

"Thanks for saying that." Bonnie smiled at both Malik and Farah. "Is there any way you can give us some cleaning supplies? I want the kids to work on this themselves. In the meantime, I'll call a carpet cleaning service who can come in and work on your stairs and the carpet in Maryanne's room. That way, the cherry stains and vomit scent should be taken care of."

The big man behind Malik shook his head. "Don't pay for a service. I can just go over to the store and pick up one of those carpet steamers. I can get this stuff cleaned up in no time."

Bonnie frowned. "That's very kind of you…I'm sorry, I don't even know your name."

"Jase. My name is Jase Drakos. Malik is my brother. And it's not all that kind. It's kind of payback for all the times that Bruno, Malik, Renzo, and I got in similar situations."

Malik grinned. "Isn't that the truth? I'd do it, but I have a teenage boy to scare when he picks up my daughter for her first date. Don't worry about this, Bonnie. It's not the end of the world."

"It really isn't," Farah assured her.

Again, Bonnie found herself biting her bottom lip. She immediately stopped. "Thank you, Jase. I'd sure appreciate that. Let me give you some money for the rental. I just need to go to the back bedroom and get my purse."

"Don't worry about it. You can take me out to lunch sometime."

"Huh?"

"What's your name?" he asked.

"Bonnie. Bonnie Larkin. Seriously, let me just go get my purse."

"It's nice to meet you, Bonnie." He held out his hand, and she reached out to shake it.

What the hell?

She did her best not to snatch her hand back. It was like she had just touched lightning. Jase gave her a wicked smile.

"He won't bite," Farah assured her. "Let him do this for you, Bonnie. And Jase, make it dinner instead of lunch. I'll even babysit."

"That's a good idea." His smile got wider. "I'd love to take you out to dinner, Bonnie."

Shit, he has a dimple, too.

No.

Not that. No liking smiles or dimples. I have kids to raise.

"That sounds great," she said weakly.

"Mom?" Amber touched her waist. "Can we go play with Punk until we start cleaning?"

"No, you may not. Get on up to Maryanne's room and wait for me."

"But it smells," Lachlan whined.

Bonnie grinned. "Yes, it does, doesn't it? Serves you right. Next time, I want you to think about the consequences before you act."

She watched as her twins started toward the stairs.

"Why is she always talking about consequences?" Lachlan asked Amber.

"I think 'cause she doesn't want us to do bigger things that turn into bigger mistakes."

"You mean we could have bigger adventures?" Lachlan asked excitedly. "Like what?"

Jase let out a loud laugh. "Damn, woman, you have your work cut out for you."

2

My God, that ass!

Jase did his absolute best not to stare, but for God's sake, he was only human.

"Lachlan, hold the bag with two hands so your sister can scrape up the cherries and vomit with the dustpan and throw it into the bag."

Jase looked at the kid as he held his nose with one hand and held the bag with the other.

"Both hands," his mother said sharply. It was the first time she had come close to raising her voice. Pretty good, all things considered.

"But it stinks," he moaned pitifully.

"If you don't think things through, most of your consequences will stink," she said patiently. "Now use both hands."

The cute blonde, with curly hair like her mom, giggled.

"Don't laugh, it's not fair, Amber," Lachlan frowned at his sister.

"I'm the one shoveling throwed-up. That's not fair." She turned her big blue eyes to her mom. "Can we change now?"

"I'll tell you what. You go sit on the top stair and wait for me. Don't go downstairs. I'll get you some food in ten minutes, but only if you stay right there. Got it?"

"Are you going to shovel up the throwed-up?" Lachlan asked.

"Yes. Then I'm going to use the vacuum that Mr. Drakos brought. After that, I'll get you some food."

Lachlan shoved the plastic bag at his mother. She took it, and her daughter handed her the dustpan. They started toward the door.

"Wait a minute." The kids stopped. "What do you need to do?"

They both turned around in unison. They smiled the cutest smiles. "Thank you for helping, Mr. Drakos," Amber said.

"Yeah. Thanks," Lachlan said.

Then they were out the door. Jase would bet his bottom dollar that they would have Farah conned into plates of food within two minutes.

Bonnie was still on her knees, and she twisted to look up at him. "I can't thank you enough. I'm sorry I wasn't finished by the time you got back with the steam cleaner, but I really thought it was important that my little terrors did most of the cleaning."

"That's how our parents always did it. Sometimes it actually sunk in," Jase said as he knelt down and tugged at the plastic bag and pan that she was holding.

"What are you doing?"

"So far you haven't got your pretty dress messed up, let's keep it that way, shall we?" Her dress had scrunched up almost to the top of her thighs, and Jase tried his best not to ogle her pretty, plump flesh. Thinking about this woman's thighs would cause too many adverse reactions at his brother's family-friendly barbecue.

"What about you in your jeans?" she protested.

"Malik and I are about the same size. I'll just grab something from him. Done deal." Jase made quick work of shoveling cherry-smelling vomit as Bonnie pulled the down comforter out of the duvet cover.

"Well, here's some good news. The comforter is fine. Nothing leaked through the duvet. I'm telling you, with these two, my dry cleaner is making her monthly rent," she laughed.

"How old are they, six?"

"Seven. They were preemies. Twins and all. Because they look younger, they'll sucker you in. You won't realize they're so devious."

"Seems like Amber is the mastermind."

"You caught that, did you?"

Her smile was positively wicked. Kind of like her son's. He enjoyed seeing that twinkle in her eye.

"How do you keep a straight face?" Jase asked.

"Most of the time, it's easy. I'm really trying to teach them right from wrong, and I want the lesson to get through at an early age. Like when they were three, but apparently, I failed. So now I'm trying for the lessons to sink in at seven," Bonnie sighed.

"And laughing?"

"I bite the inside of my lip, or pinch my hand so hard it bruises," she admitted. "I swear, they'll come up with the darndest things. Amber will mastermind something, Lachlan will put his twist on it, and now we have cherry pie dog vomit all over my friend's daughter's bedroom. I wish this were a one-off, but it isn't. You should see the science experiments they concoct, and their book reports that turn into creative writing exercises."

"Were you like this as a kid?" Jase asked.

"Me?" Bonnie folded up the duvet cover and kneeled beside him. Once again, her skirt pushed up.

Is she doing that on purpose?

He looked up to catch her expression.

Nope. She was just pushing back the dust ruffle to check under the bed. And her ass was pointing straight at him. It looked ten times better when it was five inches from his face. Bonnie twisted around with her hand out.

"Found more vomit. Can you give me the dustpan?"

"Let me." He gently shoulder-checked her to the side. "Again, you don't want to get messed up. You still have two hungry mouths to feed."

She snorted. "I'm sure they've already sweet-talked Farah into a full meal."

"And dessert?" Jase asked.

"Oh yeah, a brownie ice cream sundae, most likely."

"I'm going to stick with them at the next party."

Bonnie raised her eyebrow. "So, you like cleaning up throwed-up?" she asked, mimicking her son.

"If it gets me a brownie ice cream sundae, I do."

"Well, better get this show on the road. I'll go put this in the washer. When I'm done, I'll come back and steam this carpet."

"What are you talking about?" Jase asked. "I'm going to be cleaning the carpet. It's going to take all of five minutes, ten minutes tops. I'll probably be done by the time you get back."

"You've already helped enough." She smiled. He watched her dress hang low in front as she bent down to put on her sexy sandals. Her toes were painted the exact same color as her dress, and she had a toe ring.

How had I missed that?

As she suspected, she found Amber and Lachlan eating out at one of the patio tables, their plates heaped with food. Amber had a piece of cake beside her plate, and Lach had a piece of cherry pie next to his. She sat down next to them.

"Lachlan, cherry pie? Really?"

"That's our favorite, Mom. Mrs. Drakos will give you some."

"After all that clean-up, I don't think I'll eat cherry pie for at least a year."

"Get real," Amber said as she finished swallowing some macaroni salad. "I say you'll be eating cherry pie in less than a month."

Lachlan laughed. "She's right, Mom. Almost every time you go grocery shopping you bring home a Teeter cherry pie."

"I do not."

"Yeah, you do," Lachlan said around a full mouth of

beans. "Especially if Brandi didn't show up to work. You hate that."

"Don't talk with your mouth full," Amber and Bonnie said at the same time.

Lachlan swallowed the whole mouthful of beans and opened his mouth wide to show them both it was empty. "Now I don't have anything in my mouth, so I can keep talking."

Bonnie heard a warm chuckle behind her back. It caused a tingle all the way down her spine. A tingle like she hadn't felt in years.

"Can I get you a plate of food?"

She took a deep breath, trying to pull herself together.

Do not think about sex. No sexy thoughts. Think of him like the janitor at work. Pretend he's Melvin.

Bonnie turned around on the bench and was eye level with Jase's denim-covered crotch.

Not good.

No, good.

Sooooo, good.

Bad Bonnie.

She looked upwards.

His T-shirt was kind of tight. *Good Lord.* She could see his abs. The man had a six-pack. And she had to continue looking up and up and up and up. Over that massive chest that resulted in shoulders that looked like they could carry the weight of the world. Finally, she met bedroom eyes that told her he was aware of her minute long perusal, and he was pleased.

Get it together!

"Uh, what?"

"I asked if I could get you a plate of food. If you told me if you liked beef or chicken, and the kind of sides you like, I could set you up. That way, you could spend some quality time with your little darlings."

It took her more than a minute to figure out what to say. When he was just the guy helping her out upstairs, that was different. Now he was approaching socially. Big difference.

I don't do social!

"Mom likes cherry pie," Lachlan called out. "And she likes the macaroni with mayonnaise. And a roll, don't forget the butter. She hates it when there's no butter."

"That wasn't what he asked, Lach. Mom likes chicken and coleslaw, Mr. Drakos. That's really nice of you to get a plate for Mom. Are you going to sit with us after you get your food? We can scoot over and make room."

Was Amber flirting?

Great, I have a seven-year-old flirt on my hands.

"How about it, Bonnie? Can I get you a plate and come sit next to you? Seating is at a premium."

"That would be very nice. Jase, right?" Bonnie replied.

"Yep, my name is Jase. I'll be back in no time. He turned and took a step, then looked over his shoulder at her. Should I really get you cherry pie, all things considered?"

She sighed.

"Yes. Lach's right, it's my downfall."

Jase shook his head and chuckled. "I'll be back."

He looked just as good going as he did coming.

"So?" Farah whispered as she plopped down beside her. "What do you think of Malik's brother? He's even a helpful hottie. Right?"

"Keep your voice down. Little pitchers have big ears."

"I'm whispering. I think I wrangled you a dinner date. You're so going to owe me."

"What are you talking about? You owe me. I've done your last two color jobs for free."

"That's because you said you couldn't stand what the other stylist had done, and you forced me into your chair. Anytime you force a person to have a dye job, it's automatically free." Farah flipped back her black hair with the pretty auburn undertones.

"Well, just come to me from now on, okay?"

"How was I supposed to know you could do a black woman's hair?"

"You could do this amazing little thing called asking...?"

Farah started laughing. "Oooops, hottie ahead. Gotta go."

Jase set a plate with far too much food in front of her, then he placed a plate with three times the amount of food as hers in front of him.

"Wow. Can you really eat that much?" Lachlan asked.

Jase laughed. "Yep."

"And your tummy won't hurt?" Amber asked.

"Nope."

"Mom, are you going to eat all that?" Lachlan asked as he pointed to her plate.

"I might." Bonnie raised her eyebrow. "You've had more than enough to eat right now. Why don't you play for a while, and then you can come back and eat your dessert?"

"But you have—"

"Lachlan..." Bonnie said his name as she raised her eyebrow.

"I think I'm going to go play now. Thanks again for cleaning up the throwed-up, Mr. Drakos." He scrambled off the bench seat, then helped Amber off the bench too. "Come on, let's play croquet. They give us big hammers to hit things."

Bonnie sighed.

"Don't worry," Jase said. "Two of my teammates are over there keeping things under control." Jase pointed at two other men who were dressed very close to the way Jase was. Both were in T-shirts tight enough that a girl could see what all they had going on, and they had it all going on. Then both of them were wearing jeans and boots.

Hmm. Well, at least with those outfits, they would definitely keep the kindergartners on up to the high school kids in line. She turned her attention back to Jase.

"What do you mean, teammates? Are you on a football team or something?"

"No, we're in the Navy. We work together."

"Ahhh, Little Creek, huh?" She sighed.

"Why do you say it like that?" Jase asked right

before he took a big bite of the hamburger he had put together.

"Well, first, thanks for all that you do for our country. I mean that sincerely."

Jase continued to chew, so he nodded.

Bonnie tried to gather her thoughts. She wanted to say what she had to say and say it right.

Jase swallowed, wiped his mouth, then took a small sip of his beer.

"Okay, hit me. I'm a big boy. Six five, to be exact." His eyes twinkled, and he had a breathtaking smile.

"Okay, but I might say this wrong. Please know that I'm not painting everyone with the same brush, okay?"

"Okay," he nodded.

Bonnie bit her bottom lip. "I'm a stylist at Trinity Salon in Little Creek, right off of Independence Blvd. We take up the second floor above a lot of little shops."

"I don't think I've noticed you," Jase admitted.

"We're above the Rusty Elbow Pub."

He grinned. "Now I know exactly where you are."

"Yep, you mention that to a man in the Navy, and they clue in. I should have clocked you as a SEAL right off, but I was too busy with Amber and Lachlan's latest mission. Maybe they'll end up in Spec Ops too." She gave a weak chuckle, and Jase joined in.

"I'm thinking that if they ever team up later in life, the world better watch out," Jase said as he forked some potato salad into his mouth.

"Anyway, a lot of my clients are either former SEAL...well, I'm not sure I would classify them as girlfriends, but former SEAL flings. Then there's the other group of girls who are SEAL fling wannabes. I really think all of them are hoping to end up as wives, but that has only happened once. So, I'm stuck with the broken hearts and disillusionment as they spend hours talking in my chair. It really gets tiring. Now, before you say anything, please, please know that I realize it takes two to tango." Bonnie winced. "I totally get it. But this revolving door on both sides is disheartening, you know?"

Bonnie stared down at her food and forced herself to take a forkful of coleslaw. Once again, she'd said too much. She always said too much. At least this time she hadn't blurted. She'd thought about what she'd said. Still, she'd said too much.

Jase said nothing. He was concentrating on his meal as well. At least he didn't get up and leave. That would have been really embarrassing.

Jase cleared his throat, and Bonnie swallowed her coleslaw and looked over at him.

"I get your point." Jase tipped his chin toward the two men overseeing the croquet game. "One of those guys over there just got engaged. I've never seen someone so happy, and three other men on my team have found women they would lay down their lives for." Then he grinned. "Now, I'm not saying that some of the guys aren't busy sowing their wild oats and have probably spent a little time with your customers, but I think they're the younger members of some of the SEAL teams. If I had to guess, the women you're talking about are young as well, aren't they?"

"Mostly," Bonnie agreed. "I have a few dyed in the

wool SEAL groupies. I think their aim is to meet and greet every boy who gets their trident."

This time it was Jase's turn to wince.

"Yeah, they need touch-ups on their gray twice a month." Bonnie held back a smile.

"Well, I can see how you might be a little jaded about SEALs in general, but I think you need to understand that some of us are grownups. We're not afraid of actual relationships."

"You mean they're not afraid of throw-up?" Bonnie smiled.

"Exactly," Jase grinned.

"Good to know. I'll let some of the other stylists know that there is hope."

"But not you?"

"Jase, I'm too old to be looking."

He snorted. "Twenty-eight is not too old."

"Are you trying to flirt?" Bonnie asked as she broke apart her roll and slathered on the butter.

"You finally caught on, did you?"

"You're not very good at it. I'm twenty-five. You're not supposed to guess a woman's age, didn't you know that?"

"Fuck, Bonnie, you were just a baby when you had your babies."

"Luckily, I had wonderful role models on how to be a parent. That really helped."

"And your husband? What about him?"

"We never married. We were both young. Really young. He denied the twins were his, and his parents backed him up."

"Didn't you do a paternity test?"

"I looked things up online. If I had, he might have paid child support, but then he would have been entitled to time with my children. He didn't come from a healthy home. And I saw his true colors when he walked away when things got tough. I didn't want him around my kids."

"So, your parents helped?"

"In a way." She cocked her head. "I'm pretty sure I hear a fight between Amber and Lachlan. It was bound to happen," she said as she picked up her paper plate.

"I can take care of that," Jase said as he put his hand on hers.

Just that brief touch and her hormones roared to life. She pulled her hand away. "Thanks Jase. Time to go play referee."

THREE DAYS later he was still thinking about Bonnie, which was the reason he started his run before oh-five-hundred on a Sunday morning.

Might as well be productive if I can't sleep.

Halfway through his run, Jase pulled his cell phone out of his pocket. It was the third text he'd received this morning, and it was only oh six hundred. What was up with his family?

At least Angelica finally had the good sense to create a group text, but he still wasn't going to answer it. He was going to need the calming effects of the run before interacting with that much drama.

The hard-packed, damp sand made him feel more in tune with the world around him than when he was running on the track at base. Hell, it was even better than when he was hiking in a forest. There was just something about the beach at sunrise. Here, as he was running all-out beside the Atlantic Ocean, he felt connected to a vast universe. It soothed him.

When he felt the buzz of his phone one last time, he ignored it. But he still turned around and headed for home.

Jase grinned. Talk about being connected to something larger than himself. Yep, his family was definitely like no other family in the world.

"And we're here. Why?" Renzo asked, not bothering to take off his sunglasses. "They probably charge ten dollars for a five-ounce glass of orange juice."

"It's seven ounces, and it's twelve dollars. Don't worry, the production company is paying for it, so stop your bellyaching," Angelica said as she took a sip of her mimosa.

"You need to have your production company send themselves a fruit basket to thank themselves," Farah said as she held up her flute of champagne to toast Angelica.

"I didn't even know they had some place so fancified in Virginia Beach," Malik said as he pulled his ball cap down even lower. "Kill me now."

"You're the one who wanted to get together, just the

family," Renzo said as he grabbed a muffin out of one of the three baskets on the table. He took a bite and half of it was gone.

"You know, you could put it on your plate and butter it first. Like an actual human being?" Angelica said as she looked at her brother.

"Where would be the fun in that?" Renzo smirked at his sister.

In the corner, underneath a palm tree so he was in the shade, Jase sat back and enjoyed the show. Renzo lifted his sunglasses and sent him a look. He knew Jase was doing his best to stay in the shadows, and he was about to call him out.

Damn.

"So, Jase, Farah told me you agreed to take a pretty little thing out to dinner. I'm sure everybody here would love to know all about her."

"I'm not sure that's going to happen." Jase took a sip of coffee and waited for the shit to hit the fan.

It didn't take long.

"What are you talking about?" Farah's tone was sharp. "You agreed to take Bonnie out. I was there. I heard you."

Jase put down his coffee mug and held up his hands. "This isn't on me, it's her. You should have checked things out better. She doesn't think much of SEALs."

"What are you talking about?" Angelica said in a dramatically shocked voice.

Here it comes.

"You risk life and limb every time you leave the

country. How could she think you were anything less than a hero? What kind of snobby you-know-what did you try to fix him up with, anyway?" Angelica glared at her sister-in-law.

"Angelica, retract those claws," Malik instructed his little sister. "You know damn good and well that my wife would only set Jase up with the very best, yeah?" Angelica reluctantly nodded her head. Malik turned to Jase. "And you. Give us the entire story, not just the half that gets you out of a date."

It sucked being called out on your shit. That was what happened when you were surrounded by people who had known you for most of your life.

"I'm not sure, but I think Bonnie might have been burned in the past, but she didn't share. Anyway, she's a little jaded by some things she's seen. Mainly Little Creek's revolving door with women."

Farah snorted. "She's got that right. Just how many flowers have y'all pollinated, Jase?"

"Ewww," Angelica grimaced into her mimosa.

"What?" Farah exclaimed. "I thought that was a delicate way to put it. Much nicer than asking him how many notches he had on his bedpost."

"Farah, you're thinking of the younger guys. I grant you that the guys under twenty-five are looking for a field of flowers, but as time goes on, us older guys are looking to tend to that one perfect orchid."

"Angelica? Honey?" Renzo leaned over and whispered loud enough for everyone to hear. "Can you please call 911? Apparently, our big brother has suffered an aneurysm and needs to be rushed to the hospital."

"Oh please," Angelica waved her hand. "He's actually talking like an enlightened male. I am totally impressed."

"That's what I mean," Renzo said. "We need to get an ambulance here, stat!"

"Enough with the bullshit, Renzo," Farah growled. She turned her attention back to Jase. "Now tell us what really happened."

"I actually thought we had gotten past the bullshit of all SEALs being horndogs. But she ran away before I could get her number. I guess she wasn't interested." Jase shrugged.

"Are you trying to say you weren't interested?" Malik tipped back his ball cap so he could look at Jase. "The way she looked in that dress, her sense of humor and toe ring. Didn't do it for you, huh?"

"That's who we're talking about? The blonde with the curly hair?" Renzo asked as he sat straighter and pushed his sunglasses up on his head. "What the hell, Farah? Why didn't you set her up with me?"

"Maybe because we never know what country you're going to be in from month to month?" Farah said as she rolled her eyes.

"And I'm betting you're pollinating a different flower in each country," Angelica smirked.

"First, I've never pollinated anyone. I always use protection. And second, could you please, in the name of all that is holy, stop it with the flower analogy," Renzo said as he slid his sunglasses back over his eyes. "What's taking so long for my beer, anyway? At these prices, you'd think they'd have a fridge at every table."

Jase chuckled. "They sure have your number, bro," he grinned at Renzo.

"And yours." Renzo raised his eyebrow as he looked over at Jase.

"Not anymore," Jase disagreed. "The guys on my team are pairing up and happier than pigs in slop. I want to see what it's all about. And please note I did not use a flower analogy."

"'Preciate it." Renzo nodded his way.

The server placed tall glasses of beer in front of Renzo, Jase, and Malik. She then topped off the mimosas and champagne for the ladies. "Can I get you another bottle of champagne?" she asked.

"Yes, please," Angelica smiled as she waved her hand around the table. "We're celebrating. It's rarely so many of us get together. We need another wedding."

Jase and Renzo slid lower in their seats.

"Your meals should be here shortly. I'll bring the champagne with them." She smiled.

"If you're serious about getting serious, are wedding bells in your future?" Angelica asked Jase.

"Sis, just hold your horses. I have to date someone before that's going to happen. What about you? Every time I turn around, your name is linked to some movie star or another. When are you going to announce that you're pregnant and getting married?"

Angelica gave a sad sigh. "Everything you read is some sort of setup by my agent. I haven't been on a proper date for over a year, and that was Eric."

"That loser?" Malik asked. "Didn't Renzo have to fly

to California and help kick his ass out of your condo? Did you ever get a restraining order?"

"That would have hit the tabloids, so no. Anyway, Renzo made it quite clear that if he stepped out of line, he would demolish him. Even when Eric and I are at the same parties, he scuttles away from me and stays on the other side of the room. What's more, he hasn't said one damn word to any of the papers. I was sure he was going to whine about me kicking him out, but he didn't."

Jase leaned over and gave Renzo a fist bump. He'd been out of the country when all of that had gone down, but he'd known Renzo could and would take care of things.

"Enough about me, I want to know if you're going to let the woman with the toe ring push you to the curb," Angelica asked. "It's not like you to walk away from a challenge."

Jase grinned when three servers came to the table and started dispersing their food. He looked at his two-egg omelet, two strips of bacon, and one slice of toast. It was elegantly displayed with a purple orchid and would only put a small dent in his hunger.

Dammit, I knew I should have stopped at the taco truck and grabbed a couple of breakfast burritos before coming.

"Oh look, Jase, you have an orchid on your plate. It's an omen," Farah called out gleefully. "Now you have to take Bonnie out for dinner."

I'm doomed.

3

"Hottie alert," Shannon whispered. "I call dibs."

Bonnie didn't even bother to turn around. She concentrated on the cut she was giving to the new customer she had in her chair. The woman was a natural brunette who had warm caramel highlights from the sun. Her thick hair had been three inches past her shoulders, and it hadn't been doing her any favors. Bonnie had been doing razor cuts for the last eighteen months, and her customer had been a perfect candidate.

She was almost done cutting the long hair so that it feathered in the front, highlighting the woman's striking eyes and high cheekbones. She turned her around in the chair.

"What do you think?" Bonnie asked.

The woman stared and said nothing for almost a minute. For a moment, Bonnie worried she had made a mistake.

"Oh my God, I love it. I look like a whole new woman. This is phenomenal."

Bonnie smiled. "I'm glad you like it."

"Seriously, I've never looked so good after a haircut. I can't possibly thank you enough." The woman touched her hair, then turned from side to side. Bonnie handed her a mirror and turned her around in the chair.

"Check out the back. See if that's what you wanted."

"I love it," she enthused.

"That's what I wanted to hear," Bonnie smiled. "I hope you'll come back and see me."

"How often should I come back for a cut to maintain this?"

"Probably every six to eight weeks."

"Great, I'll book it now," the woman said as she got out of the chair. Bonnie was taken aback when the woman pulled her in for a hug. That didn't happen too often, but she had to grin. Even better, she left a twenty-five percent tip in cash.

After the lady left to go pay up front, Bonnie policed her area, sweeping up the hair on the floor and making sure her chair was clean and everything was put away the way she liked. She looked at her schedule for the day and grinned. She had forty-five minutes to kick back before her next appointment. It had been a busy morning, so a break would be wonderful. She could slip out and grab a bubble tea from the shop downstairs.

"Hey, Shannon, I've got a break. Do you want a bubble tea?"

"I don't think you do, sweets. I went up front to grab Mr. Hotterson. He said he was waiting for you. How'd you score him? Have you been holding out on your girl?"

Shannon's station had a better view of the lush lobby, which was fine by Bonnie. It meant that she kept focused on her clients. Shannon was a lovely woman and had been a stylist for over twenty years. Bonnie had learned a lot from her in the five years she had worked at Trinity Salon, but she tended to interrupt too much when Bonnie had a client in the chair. She'd addressed it a few times, but it hadn't sunk in. Now Bonnie just ignored her like she was part of the music that the salon played. Amazingly, Shannon took no offense.

"Well, I better go get my new client. Are you sure he's not a regular customer? It's odd that he would ask for me as a new request."

"Trust me, I would have remembered something that pretty sitting in your chair before. Even if he came in on one of my days off, everybody would have mentioned him, and Clare would have taken a couple of pics when he wasn't looking."

Bonnie shuddered. Clare was always pulling that kind of bullshit. Bonnie could only hope that the young woman would grow out of that kind of behavior. She headed to the front of the salon, a professional smile on her face. Her steps faltered as she saw Jase Drakos thumbing through Vogue magazine, looking comfortable as could be. He was the only man sitting in the lobby, so she knew he was the man who was her client.

"Hi Jase," she said in her most professional manner.

He set down his magazine and took a moment to look at her, from her head to her toes, then back up to her eyes. Her blood heated every second he took perusing her.

Bad girl.

"Hello, Bonnie," he said as he stood up and walked toward her. "It's nice to see you again. I noticed I needed a haircut, and I realized we didn't have time to finish our conversation last weekend. The coincidence was too obvious for me to pass up, so here I am."

Damn. That smile.

Bonnie rolled her eyes. "Coincidence, huh?"

"Absolutely."

"I don't remember telling you what salon I worked at."

"You told me it was above the Rusty Elbow."

"Oh yeah, I did."

"And luckily, they told me you have time available. I'd say it's kismet, wouldn't you?"

"Uhm."

Shit, now I'm sounding like Lachlan.

"Bonnie, are you going to take him back to your station, or should I assign another stylist?" The woman behind the front desk asked.

God, Lorelei stomped on her last nerve. She was constantly trying to cause rifts between the stylists, and Bonnie was pretty sure that she purposely gave some of the higher paying clients to the stylists she liked best, but she hadn't been able to prove it.

Jase stepped up to the counter. "Bonnie and I are old friends. I only want to have my hair cut by her. Can you write that down, honey?"

"I'll need your last name to enter it into the system, and I'll also need your phone number," Lorelei bit out.

"No, you'll just need my name," Jase corrected her. "Jase Drakos." He spelled out his name, and Bonnie tried not to giggle as Lorelei gritted her teeth.

Fuck, there was just too much to like about this guy. He even caught onto petty girl shit and shut it down.

"Why don't you follow me?" Bonnie suggested with a smile.

"I would love to."

For the very first time, she wished she was wearing high heels so there would be a little more sway in her walk. Oh well, it was what it was.

Jase started to sit down in her chair.

"Hold on," Bonnie said as she bent down to pull out a cape from the cupboard beside her station. She unfolded it and gave it a good snap so that it opened and she could wrap it around him. As soon as she had it ready, she realized she had a problem.

A big problem.

A six-foot-five-inch problem.

"Jase, can I get you to crouch down a little so I can wrap this around you?"

He looked over his shoulder and smirked. "How about I just put this on myself?"

It was the smirk that did it.

"How about you just do as I asked?" she retorted in her PTA voice.

"Touchy little thing, aren't you?" He grinned as he crouched low enough so she could pull the wrap around him and fasten it in the back. He stood back up.

"Now what, boss?"

"Now you sit down and tell me what you're hoping to accomplish with your haircut today."

"I'm hoping that the haircut lasts long enough to talk you into having dinner with me tomorrow night."

"Bonnie, that's a fantastic line," Shannon interrupted. "You should definitely let him take you out to dinner."

"See, she agrees." Jase gifted Shannon with a toothpaste commercial worthy smile.

"How about I start cutting your hair and you try to convince me, hmm?" Bonnie asked Jase's reflection in the mirror.

"Seems fair."

"Now, what do you want me to do with your hair?"

"It tends to curl when it gets too long. If you could chop enough off so it doesn't curl for the next five weeks, I'd be a happy man."

Bonnie ran her fingers through his hair, just like she did with all her clients with short hair, trying to get an idea of the texture, thickness and where the part was. But as she again speared her fingers through his strands of hair, she felt her heart speed up as she enjoyed the coarse texture of his hair and the way the waves melted through her fingertips.

"Well?"

"Hmm?"

"What's the diagnosis? Will I live?"

Bonnie looked at Jase in the mirror and she could see herself blushing.

Dammit.

"I think you'll survive." Her smile was forced. "You really only need about an inch off the sides and back, and maybe a half inch off the top."

"But Doc, what about in the front? It's important that I can see. If I run into something that requires a second or third look, I'd hate for my vision to be impaired."

Bonnie rolled her eyes. "Does this kind of drivel work with women?"

Jase winked at her. "Ninety-five percent of the time. Are you telling me you're the five percent it doesn't work with?"

"Yep."

"Well, that just means I'm going to have to up my game. What's more, I have Farah rooting for me, so I can always ask her for advice."

"A thirty-seven-year-old man has to go ask his sister-in-law for advice on how to get a woman to go out to dinner with him? What *has* the world come to?" she teased.

"I caught that, you know?" he said, lifting his left eyebrow.

"Caught what?"

"You know how old I am. You must have asked a couple of questions about me. What else did you ask?"

Bonnie closed her eyes for a moment, knowing she had been caught and needing strength.

"I might have asked how many girlfriends you've brought to these family and friends' barbecues. She said that the only one you ever brought was your fiancée, and you broke up four or five years ago."

"Why'd you ask that question? Were you interested if I belonged to the babe of the month club?"

"Something like that," Bonnie ruefully admitted. Bonnie blew her bangs up out of her face, then looked him dead in the eye. "And if I were totally truthful, I really appreciated your help that afternoon when you got the steamer. I was so frazzled all I could think of was getting a carpet cleaner in as soon as possible. You were a lifesaver."

"I saw the way you were handling things. You would have figured it out," he assured her.

"I'm not sure, and I would have hated for Maryanne to have a stinky bedroom overnight." She placed her hand on his broad shoulder. "Okay, time to get up and go to the shampoo station."

Jase frowned. "I had a shower before I came. I washed my hair then."

"This is all part of the service. Also, I have to cut your hair when it's wet."

"Damn, this sure isn't like when I go to the place next to the liquor store."

She smiled. "I get that a lot." She tapped his shoulder. "Now get moving, chop, chop. I have another client in thirty minutes."

Jase got up and easily followed her, even though she

was rushing to get to the shampoo bowls in the back room where everything was calm and relaxed for their clients.

"Bonnie," Shannon called out before she opened the door to the back room. "You know that Mrs. Lyles is always late. You can take your time. God knows I would."

Jase's chuckle from behind her tickled her senses. She opened the door and ushered him in. The lighting was low, and they had Gregorian chants playing softly in the background.

"Here we are. Let me put a towel around your neck, over your cape, so water doesn't drip and your collar gets wet."

"Uhm, Bonnie, I'm wearing a T-shirt and jeans. I don't think my collar getting wet is going to be an issue, seeing as how it's a T-shirt."

Bonnie thumped her fists on her hips and shook her head. "Even where you normally get your hair cut they must put a towel around you so when they cut your hair, you're not covered in clippings."

Jase held up his hands in surrender. "You're right. This is your area of expertise. I won't second-guess you again."

"Yes, you will," Bonnie muttered under her breath. "Now, it's time for you to relax," she said louder, in her most professional tone. Normally, she talked in a soothing and relaxing tone, but it was going to take more than a minute for her to be able to do that. Maybe when the warm water started flowing and she could smell the herb-scented shampoo, then she could relax.

Jase sat down in the chair.

"Do you want me to put your feet up?" She pointed to the lever on the side of the chair that would raise the footrest.

"I think we can skip that," he chuckled. "Is there always new age music playing in this room?"

"Yes. This is an area where we like our clients to relax and enjoy their experience before we take them back onto the main floor."

"So, the main floor is where you get me to spill my guts, right?"

"You've got it. Think of me as your bartender slash therapist."

Jase chuckled a little longer this time.

His laugh got to her. It had when she'd been at Farah and Malik's house, too. It was a genuine laugh, and it tasted like caramel, and it hit her solar plexus like a gong. It reverberated throughout her body.

Snap out of it.

She grabbed two heated towels and rolled them up and put them under his neck. "How does this feel?" She purposely lowered her voice so that he could relax. "Are you comfortable, or are the two towels too much, or not enough?"

"You did it just right, Bonnie."

She smiled at his praise.

She walked behind the shampoo bowl and turned the nozzle, then tested the water on her wrist until she got it to a pleasing heat level.

"When I start, let me know if it gets too hot or too cold."

"Right now, you're putting off just the right amount of heat," he rumbled.

God, give me strength.

Bonnie took the nozzle and started at his hairline. She used her free hand to massage water into the top of his scalp. She knew he liked the heat level because she watched his shoulders relax just a little.

Let's see how much further I can get him to relax.

She continued to wet his thick hair, careful not to get any water into his ears. Finally, she reached the nape of his neck, and she used a stronger pressure to ensure every strand of his hair was soaked, and that she could feel his rock-tight muscles relax just a smidgeon. That was when he closed his eyes.

Bonnie turned off the water and went to the shelf with an array of different shampoos. She chose the one with earthy tones of cypress, leather, and bergamot. It wasn't too overpowering, but it was a scent she rarely used. It was a scent she associated with strength, and most men who she worked on just didn't have the aura of strength that Jase did.

She opened the bottle and breathed it in.

So good.

She went back to Jase. She poured a good-sized portion in her hand, then threaded it through his wet hair. The scent wafted up and surrounded her as she built up a lather. When all the suds had been evenly distributed, Bonnie began the mindless work of massaging Jase's head. This was one of her favorite things to do for a client. She'd read up on it and asked her friend Lucy, who worked at a chiropractic office, for some tips on how to really give a good scalp massage.

Bonnie always took the time to do it right. She worked on the back of Jase's neck, above the heated towels, making sure the lather was properly worked in and her fingers tenderly pushed in while her thumbs swirled around to the sides of his neck. It was important to never go too hard. Her job was to ensure he was relaxed, not to hurt him.

Her hands drifted upwards until her fingers stroked around the shell of his ear. He had gorgeous ears. Many people didn't, but Jase's ears were perfect. She wanted to pinch and bite his earlobe.

Bad Bonnie.

Bad.

She speared her fingers through his thick hair and took a deep breath of all the scents, the cypress. The bergamot. The leather. Then she smelled something else. It was tantalizing. She couldn't place it. She should be able to. She worked with scents all the damn time. There was a bit of spice. She wanted to nuzzle his neck, breathe in his scent, revel in it.

Bad Bonnie. But it would be oh so good.

Shannon opened the door to the shampoo room. "Hey, toots, I can take Mrs. Lyles if you want…"

"What time is it?"

"Ten to two. You're going to have to hustle if you want to make it to her normal arrival time."

"Thanks Shannon. You don't have anything?"

"Nope."

"Let me see how it goes. Just be my back-up, okay?"

"Absolutely. Happy to finally do you a solid."

JASE DIDN'T WANT to do anything to stop Bonnie from massaging his head. Whatever shampoo she was using smelled outstanding. Not as good as Bonnie smelled, but still, pretty damned good. He never considered shampoo before. There was the stuff that his dad had used, or the stuff that was on sale, or when he was really in a pinch, he used a bar of Irish Spring. But this stuff was the shit.

"You doing, okay?"

She even sounded different. Her voice was lower. It was like she was using her sex voice, that voice that all women had when they were picking a guy up in a bar. But that's not what Bonnie was doing. This voice was smoky, and it was turning him on like crazy. Thank God he was wearing this goddamn cape. He was picturing her in his bedroom, using that smoky voice, and it was driving him out of his mind.

"I'm doing great," he finally answered her. "Any better, and I would have melted right into the chair."

Except my penis. That would have been the one thing that wouldn't have melted. It would have been a rock-hard column standing straight up in a pool of goo.

"I'm glad." He could hear that she was telling the truth. He liked that.

"I need to rinse your hair, then I can get you back to my station."

The idea of being back out on the floor with all

those chattering people, instead of here where it was just the two of them, made him cranky.

"Does anyone hire you just to give them weekly shampoos?"

Bonnie laughed. "You're kidding, right? Who would do something like that?"

"Me. You have magic in your fingers."

Jase caught her gaze and saw that she was blushing. Good, he was getting to her. That's what he wanted. If she was off kilter a bit, then he could get under her defenses.

"Just lie back, and I'll get your hair rinsed."

Jase closed his eyes, savoring her touch as she sifted her small fingers through his hair, underneath the warm water.

"It's not too hot or too cold, is it?"

He heard the concern in her voice. It tugged at a part of him he didn't know was there. It felt good.

"It's perfect, Bonnie."

"That's good." He heard the smile in her voice.

She turned off the water and actually found another warm towel to dry his hair. Talk about being pampered.

"Okay, Big Guy, let's get you back to my chair and see if I can live up to your expectations."

As he sat up, he looked over his shoulder at her. "Trust me, Bonnie. You have surpassed all of my expectations here in the salon. I can't imagine what it will be like when we go out to dinner."

She was so fair skinned; he could see her blush as it

started on her upper chest and crept up her neck, then settled on her cheeks.

"Who said we're having dinner?"

"Farah did. You can't back out on me. If you do, then not only will I catch hell, so will Malik. Do you really want to do that to us?"

"I'll make her understand it was my decision."

Jase raised his eyebrow. "Do you really think that's going to work?"

Bonnie's shoulders slumped. "No. I don't."

"What's the harm in the two of us going to dinner? And in retribution, we arm Lachlan with a cherry pie and Amber with a vat of chocolate pudding when we drop them off with Farah to babysit."

He grinned when she burst out with a giggle.

"You're right, that could be fun," she said while still giggling.

"All's fair."

She had a mischievous grin on her face when she sat him down in her salon chair. He liked it. She'd shown her sense of humor a few times at his brother's house, but she'd quickly hidden it when she was trying to be the grown-up in front of her children. Or when she felt like he was interested in her. But now, she was just being herself, and she was just too cute for words.

"What are you thinking?" Bonnie asked as she got out her comb and shears.

"Nothing."

"That's a pretty broad smile, for nothing."

Jase's smile got even bigger. "I'm trying to think of where to take you for dinner. And for our second date,

I'm trying to think about where Amber and Lachlan might like to go. That isn't the big mouse pizza place, is it?" Jase shuddered.

"Don't make me laugh when I have shears in my hand," she admonished.

He watched as she concentrated. But she wasn't concentrating hard. He could tell she was in the zone, but still taking in the world around her. She was aware of his expressions in the mirror, who was coming onto the main floor and what Shannon was saying beside her. She'd make an excellent operator.

She made three more decisive cuts, then shook her head and looked him dead in the eye. "What is going through your head, Mr. Drakos?"

"Nothing, I swear."

"You shouldn't swear when you say nothing. You should only say, 'I swear', when it's actually true, otherwise you'll run out of your get out of jail free cards. So, fess up. What are you thinking so hard about?"

"You."

Bonnie rolled her eyes heavenward, then rested one of her hands on each shoulder, one with the comb, the other with the shears.

"Jase, Jase, Jase. There are so many other women who would be ecstatic to have you thinking about them."

"Hear, hear! Pick me," Shannon muttered just loud enough for him and Bonnie to hear.

"Don't you have a brush to clean?" Bonnie asked. She was clearly grumpy. It just made her cuter.

"Nope. My station is neat and tidy. But thanks for your concern." Shannon beamed.

Jase worked hard to keep a straight face.

"Are you trying not to laugh?" Bonnie asked as she pointed the shears at his reflection.

"No, ma'am," he said before he burst out laughing. After he settled, he started talking while she cut his hair. "So, is there anything you don't like? Sushi, for example."

"I like sushi. I'm kind of sick of fish sticks and tater tots. But we're not going out to dinner."

"And your kids, I'm thinking first we go someplace where we could burn off a little energy before they have to sit down for dinner. Maybe that putt putt golf and games. We start with the batting cages where they both work on hitting the balls, and Lachlan can hit them as hard as he wants before we move to the putt-putt course where he's going to need a little more finesse. Then we can go to an Italian place I know that serves macaroni and cheese and a side of meatballs for the kids, and we can get adult food. How does that sound?"

Bonnie had slowly stopped cutting his hair. She was taking in everything he was saying. Her eyes lit up when he'd mentioned that Lachlan would be less likely to hit the golf ball hard if they did the batting cages first. Then she started smiling when he mentioned the macaroni and cheese.

I've got her.

"That wouldn't be any fun for you," she protested.

"Are you kidding? I'm at the putt-putt course so often, they know my name."

"Why?"

"Gustavo's kids. He's one of my brothers. He's a surgeon in Norfolk, his wife works as a physical therapist. When they need a break, I have their three boys come stay with me for a long weekend."

"How old are they?"

"The oldest is your kid's age. Then there is Ricky, he's five, and Bobby, he's four."

"That's a lot to handle."

"Yeah, but I love it. I have a big enough place for them to be comfortable, and the backyard is all fenced in so they can play, and I don't have to worry too much."

As they continued to talk, Bonnie had gone back to cutting his hair.

"Lean forward," she instructed him. "I want to clean up your neck."

She bent and reached into a low drawer. Once again, Jase got a good view of her delectable ass. He wanted to grip it. Kiss it. Bite it.

She stood up and turned around. She had the trimmer. "I need to clean-up your neck," she explained.

Jace leaned forward and Bonnie ruffled his hair. Her small hands felt good.

Bonnie sifted her fingers through the hair on the back of his head and tugged upwards. Jase could imagine her tugging at his hair as if they were in bed together. She applied the trimmer to his neck and he could feel her careful confidence.

"Sit back up."

He did.

"All done."

The only thing that made those words somewhat okay was that she had to bend down to put the shears back down in her drawer.

She pulled out a blow dryer, then she turned it on and warm air gently blew the shavings off his head, neck, and the cape.

She put her blow dryer back in the cupboard and brought out a bottle.

"What's that?" Jase asked.

"Product. I mean gel. It'll help your hair stay in place."

Jase laughed. "I think we can forego the product."

She slowly smiled. "Yeah, I can kind of see where you're not a hair gel kind of guy."

"I take enough shit from my family and teammates as is. No need setting myself up for more."

She let out a low laugh. "Now we're done." She unsnapped the cape and pulled it off.

"Nope, 'fraid not, beauty. We're not. We didn't nail down the dates and times for the dates. How about this Friday?"

"I work late on Friday, then I work early on Saturday. See, this just won't work. What with my schedule and my kids, dating is just impossible."

"Thursday would be perfect," Shannon interjected. "She only works four hours in the morning, and Friday she comes in late, so you can have a long, leisurely date on Thursday."

Bonnie turned and growled at Shannon. "And who am I going to get to watch the kids at the last minute?"

"Me." Shannon said succinctly.

"Farah." Jace answered with a smile.

They'd both answered at the same time.

Bonnie threw up her hands. "I told you. My life is too complicated to date. Plus, your life is too complicated to date. And I don't want to be just another notch on your belt."

"Lady, I haven't 'dated' or anything else with a woman," Jase used air quotes to get his point across, "for the last twelve months. I would really like to spend some time with you and get to know you. Get to know your kids. What's so wrong with that?"

"I don't want my kids hurt."

"Bonnie, I'm going to be like Malik, just another friend of the family. I will not be some man their mother is going out with, okay?"

He watched as she closed her eyes, then tipped her head heavenward.

"Okay. A date. One date."

"Two. One just you and me, then another at the game zone."

"God deliver me," she sighed. "Okay, two."

"This Thursday. Nineteen hundred hours? What's your address?"

"I'm only giving this to you because Farah trusts you." Bonnie rattled off her address, and he plugged it into his phone.

"Telephone number?"

"Why do you need to know that?" she asked suspiciously.

"I might run late, and I'd like to let you know."

She sighed, then she gave it to him.

Jase turned around to the mirror and looked at his now-dry hair. "This haircut looks outstanding. I don't know what you did exactly. It kind of looks the same, but it looks a hundred times better."

Bonnie grinned. "*That* is the magic."

4

Bonnie was on a three-way FaceTime call with Bradley and Shannon as she pulled clothes out of her closet.

"When I asked him what the dress code was, he said that he'd be wearing slacks, and I should take it from there. Whatever the fuck that means. Dammit, people, he's already seen me in the only good dress I own," she whined.

"Bullshit. Don't tell me you wear the same thing over and over again to Malik and Farah's barbecues." Bradley scolded her.

"I don't. Normally, I wear shorts and tank tops. But Farah insisted I dress up."

Bonnie pulled another dress out of her wardrobe.

"Shit. This won't work."

"Let me see," Shannon demanded.

Bonnie turned the phone around. "Oh, right, you wore that to Mrs. Anders' funeral. That's a no go. Do you have a skirt?"

"You know I do. Management asks us to wear a skirt whenever we have some fancy stylist come in to teach us stuff that we already know."

"And you wore a hoochie skirt that one time. I remember now." Shannon had the gall to giggle.

"It wasn't my fault. I forgot to wear one, and Iris gave me one of hers that she had in the back. Then she insisted I keep it. I think she thought I had cooties."

"Bonnie can't wear a hoochie skirt on her first date," Bradley interjected.

"It's not really a hoochie skirt. It almost hits her knees. It's just the way it hugs her ass. Do you do squats or something?" Shannon asked.

"I'm constantly cleaning up things around the house. Trust me, that's a workout."

"Try it on," Bradley demanded. "Put one of your tank tops on with it," he ordered. Then he paused. "I know, the bright blue one, and tuck it in."

"Then I'll be nothing but boobs and ass," Bonnie complained.

"Just do what I say. Uncle Bradley has an idea," Bradley countered.

"I'll trust you… just this once."

Bonnie shimmied into the skirt, then found the tank top in her dresser and pulled it on, tucking it in, just as Bradley had commanded.

"Done!"

"Turn the phone around so we can get a good look."

Bonnie turned it.

"No, no, no. Stand in front of the full-length mirror, then point it there," Bradley sighed in annoyance.

I'm the one who should be annoyed.

"See, I told you, nothing but ass and boobs." Bonnie turned from side to side.

"Now what about that frothy light blue blouse that you bought when we were at the farmer's market because you felt sorry for that girl who hadn't made a sale all day?"

"What in the hell am I going to do with that?" Bonnie was running out of time. Jase was going to be there soon.

"Just trust me," Bradley insisted again.

It took more than a minute to find the blouse that he'd been talking about. It was beautiful, but who in the hell was ever going to wear a see-through blouse? What's more, it would never button over her boobs.

"I've got it. I'm putting it on before you bitch at me."

"Now she looks like a hoochie in a pretty see-through sack," Shannon piped up.

"I want you to go pull that wide silver belt off your black dress. The one that you think the skirt is too short."

Bonnie rolled her eyes again, but did what her friend told her to do. She put it around the gauzy blouse.

"Holy shit. How'd you know to do that?" Bonnie wanted to know. "It covers all my assets, but still hints at them. I no longer look like I'm planning on asking him home for the evening to steal his wallet."

"It's more than that. You look classy," Shannon grinned.

"Now for the heels part of our adventure." Bradley said with glee.

Bonnie groaned. She was so used to wearing nurse shoes at the salon that high heels were murder on her feet. But she did like how they made her legs look.

"Stop it. I know you have some cute high heels. I know you shop for shoes and purses when you're depressed," Shannon said.

"Truth," Bradley chimed in. "Hold the phone so we can see you, the honey pot."

Bonnie reluctantly showed them what was on offer.

"Stop!" Shannon screeched.

"You're right, Shannon. Those are perfect."

Bonnie knew they were talking about her silver shoes. She'd found them at the outlet mall, and they were seventy-five percent off the outlet price and she couldn't resist. She had only worn them around the house when the kids were at school.

So, shoot me. It's fun feeling sexy sometimes.

"Bonnie, you're wearing those tonight. No whining. No bitching. No, nothing. Now grab them off the shelf and show us the purse you bought to go with the shoes. You are not taking your mom purse on a date."

"My purse is pretty," she defended. It was blue and perfect. Okay, the leather was frayed, and she'd had it for four years, but everything fit in it.

"It's the size of a diaper bag," Shannon scoffed. "I want to see something pretty and silver," she demanded.

"How will I fit everything I need in my silver handbag?" Bonnie asked as she bit her lip.

"Ah-ha, you *do* have one! Show it to us," Shannon cooed.

Bonnie reluctantly pushed back some of her skirts and pants and showed them the wall where all of her purses were hanging. Every one of them was a screaming deal. This was for her pretend life. Every month, she squirreled away five percent of her tips to splurge on herself. Sometimes it was for a pedicure, sometimes it was for a couple of drinks with her friends, and sometimes it was for the outlet mall.

She'd learned that from her mother. She'd had cookie jar money that was just for her. Besides working as a teacher, she made and sold beautiful quilts, and that money went into the cookie jar so she could splurge on herself. Bonnie would sometimes catch her dad putting money in the cookie jar.

God, I miss them.

"Did you hear what I said? You don't have much time left. You still have to do your hair and make-up. I think smokey eye, what do you think, Shannon?"

"Okay, you two. Thanks for all the advice, but I've got it from here."

"You better send us a picture of how you look when you're done," Bradley demanded.

"I want a picture of how Jase looks. I've only seen him in jeans and a T-shirt. I'm betting he cleans up really well," Shannon sighed.

"Later. Thanks for all of your help."

Bonnie disconnected the call and slipped on the shoes. She'd better get some more practice in before they went out. She went into the small bathroom that was connected to her bedroom. It was one of the selling points of this house when she'd bought it. That and the fact that she could afford the down payment and still feed her kids after paying the mortgage every month.

As usual, she was only wearing mascara. After having gotten her cosmetology license and working at a high-end salon in Norfolk, Virginia, she got burned out on making women look like someone they weren't, when they were really beautiful to begin with.

Still, if she went out on the date with no make-up at all, she worried Jase would think she wasn't trying. So, she did a compromise—eyeliner, mascara, a little swoosh of color on her brows so she looked like she had some instead of her blonde brows that faded into her face. She ended everything with a little bit of tinted lip gloss.

The doorbell rang.

Here goes nothing.

"DID YOU LOOK THROUGH YOUR PEEPHOLE?" Jase asked as she opened her door.

"It's seven o'clock, so I knew it was you," Bonnie answered as she motioned for him to come in.

"It's not safe for you not to use your peephole."

"I always do when the kids are home with me. And I have the deadlock set up real high so they can't reach it and open the door."

She looked gorgeous, all legs, ass, and tits. And

she'd had a killer smile until he'd started talking about her safety.

"Bonnie, you look gorgeous."

"I just need to change out purses, and I'll be ready to go." Her voice was frosty.

"I was just worried about your safety." He went over to the kitchen table where she was grabbing things from a huge purse and putting them into a tiny silver clutch. When he saw her take out cash and credit cards from her wallet, he reached out and touched the back of her hand.

"You won't need that tonight. I've got you covered."

She moved away from him and finished putting the cash and credit cards into her clutch. "Nothing personal, Jase, but if you turn into even more of an ass, I want to be able to pay for my half of the dinner and a cab to take me home."

He threw back his head and laughed.

She scowled at him. "What's so damned funny?"

"If any of my teammates heard how hard you're busting my chops, I wouldn't stop hearing about it for ten years."

"Poor you," Bonnie said as she closed her clutch with a decisive click.

"Bonnie, can I start over?" he requested softly.

He stood there watching her as her blue eyes assessed him. "I'll give you one do-over."

"One each date?" he asked hopefully.

"No. Just this once."

"I am so screwed. I make a lot of mistakes."

"Then, you should stop."

Jase had to bite the inside of his lip to keep from laughing. He'd heard her use the same tone of voice with Lachlan and Amber.

"Okay, let's pretend you've checked the peephole and opened the door."

Bonnie rolled her eyes. "Fine, I checked the peephole."

"I would then look at all that is you. From those blonde curls of yours that don't seem to want to stay up, to your beautiful face, with your big eyes and kissable lips. Then I would see you in your outfit that makes you look both sexy and fragile. My eyes would travel down to your feet and see you in shoes that have me thinking of you wearing just those when I finally get you into my bed."

Jase saw her pupils dilate and the pulse in her neck beat twice—like it had when she was angry with him.

"After I saw just how beautiful you were, I would reach out," Jase reached out and grasped her right hand. "Like this. And I would kiss the inside of your wrist," he kissed the inside of her wrist. She had such soft skin, and he felt her shiver. "Then I would tell you how grateful I am that you decided to go out on a date with me."

This time it was Bonnie who threw back her head and laughed. She pulled her hand out of his grip. "My God, man, you are one smooth operator."

It took him a moment to stop thinking about how her skin felt beneath his lips. How tantalizing her fragrance was. Jase shrugged. "Blame it on my Peruvian brother, Renzo. He swears by the inside-the-wrist kiss." Jase smiled.

Bonnie fanned her face, then looked up at him. "You have earned your way out of the doghouse. I will chuckle over this for weeks to come."

"So, you're assuming that nothing I said was true?" Jase lifted his eyebrow.

"Pretty much. Are you ready to go?"

"Not quite yet. You do realize just how beautiful you are, don't you?" His question was serious.

"Jase, I said you're out of the doghouse. Now come on, let's go. We don't want to miss our reservation." She stopped and bit her lip. "Not that we need to go someplace that requires reservations."

He heard the resignation in her voice. Just what kind of asshole men had she been dating?

"You're right, we don't want to be late. I asked for a table on the terrace overlooking the water. You might want to bring a wrap. But now that I'm thinking about it, I totally screwed up."

Bonnie tilted her head. "What do you mean?"

"I'm liking how you look and would prefer this view a hell of a lot more than any beach view. Maybe I should call and change to a table inside."

She gave him a startled look, then a smile blossomed on her face.

Now she's beginning to believe me. Good.

"Hold on and I'll get a coat."

"You do that, but I'm calling the restaurant to see if we can get an inside table with a view. You can look outside while I stare at you."

"Has anyone ever told you that you're a goof?"

"It has been mentioned," Jase said with a smile.

While she went and grabbed her coat, Jase made his call. Bonnie came back with a black trench coat. She put it over her arm. "I'm ready."

"Let's go." He opened her front door and ushered her out with a smile. He watched her carefully as she locked her door.

"You know, I am capable of locking my door by myself. I don't require a supervisor."

"I'm sorry. I didn't mean to make you feel like I was questioning your abilities. I just wanted to watch what key you were using, so I could unlock it if necessary."

"Why would it be necessary?"

"In my line of work, you're trained to expect the unexpected, so I always try to learn things."

"That much vigilance must make you tired," Bonnie said as she dropped her keys into her clutch.

He smiled down at her as he placed his hand on her lower back as they went down her walkway to the sidewalk.

"It doesn't make me tired. It keeps me on my toes. Don't you feel more on your game when you're watching Amber and Lachlan and trying to figure out their next moves?"

Bonnie looked up at him, a hint of a smile on her face. "It is kind of fun. The way their minds work is amusing, scary, and psychotic. I can't tell if they are little geniuses in the making or if they are going to grow up to be criminal masterminds."

Before he could ask a follow-up question, they were at his car.

"This is yours? I was expecting a truck."

"The truck is at home. I figured since we were going someplace nice, I wouldn't make you hoist yourself up into the passenger seat. I now see my mistake," he said as he opened the door of his Mustang.

After he made sure she was tucked inside, he closed the door. He went around the front and got in, then started the car.

"What was your mistake?" she asked as he made his way out of her neighborhood.

At a stop sign, he glanced over at her and grinned. "If I had taken my truck, I would have been able to lift you into it, which meant I would have been able to touch you a lot sooner than you're probably going to let me."

Bonnie giggled.

Yep, a giggle.

"You've got that right."

WHEN JASE PULLED into the valet at *Tease*, Bonnie was impressed. The restaurant had just opened last year, and from what she'd heard, it already had a month-long waiting list.

"How'd you get reservations so fast?" Bonnie asked.

"One of my teammates' cousins is a sous chef here. He worked us in."

Her car door was opened by one of the valets and he held out his hand to help her out of her seat.

"Thank you," she smiled up at him.

When they got to the hostess station, they were immediately taken to their table. The hostess walked them up a couple of steps, and then seated them at an inside table overlooking the water. It was a fantastic view.

"Your server will be with you shortly," she said as she handed them their menus and wine lists.

"One of my customers was raving about this place. Thank you for arranging this, Jase."

"You're welcome. I don't know what your customer told you, but I've heard that besides the seafood being great, the beef is superb."

"Good to know. I'm thinking you're talking about something other than hamburger patties?"

"You're right, I don't think hamburgers or fish sticks are on the menu," Jase chuckled. "How are the kids? Are they okay being watched by Farah and Malik?"

"Oh yeah. Both of them let Lachlan and Amber get away with too much. Too much screen time, too much junk food and they get to stay up way past their bedtime. They love it. The only good thing was that I got them to do their Friday homework before Farah picked them up."

"What grade are they in? Second?"

"Yep. Good guess. Do you have kids?"

"Nope, never been married, only engaged, and no kids."

A young girl came and brought them a basket of

warm bread and filled their water glasses. Then their server came to take their orders. Bonnie winced. "I still don't know what I want, do you, Jace?"

"No, I don't either. Can you give us a few more minutes?"

"Absolutely," he said before walking away.

"I guess we better look at the menu," Bonnie smiled. She did an internal wince at the prices. Some of the Japanese beef was going for over one hundred and fifty dollars!

"What are you feeling like? Beef or seafood?" Jase asked.

"Beef," Bonnie answered honestly. Now it was time to figure out something that wouldn't break the bank. He was in the Navy, for goodness' sake. He couldn't be making much money.

"I've got an idea, if you're willing to share," Jase said with a twinkle in his eye.

Bonnie practically sighed with relief. "I would love to share."

"Great. Can you pick out two sides?"

"Is there any side you don't want?"

"Anything sounds good to me, baby."

Bonnie quickly checked out the wine list and found the cheapest glass of red wine to go with the beef option. The glass was thirty-five dollars. Heck, there were three bottles of wine that were over a thousand dollars. Who in this world had that much money to spend?

When their waiter came back to the table, Jase

ordered Dorothy's lager. The waiter turned to her and asked her what she would like to drink. "Water's fine."

"Are you sure?" Jase asked.

"I'm not a big drinker," she smiled.

"Okay. In that case, we're ready to order our entrée. Bonnie, how do you like your meat cooked?"

"Medium to medium rare."

"Can we get the Chateaubriand medium rare, and whatever sides the lady chooses?"

Fuck!

Jase just ordered something that was more than the Japanese beef! At least the sides were reasonably priced, but seriously, shouldn't they come as part of the meal?

"We'll take the asparagus and the Yukon Gold potato cakes," she added.

Bonnie felt her palms begin to sweat. She hated the idea of Jase going to so much trouble on a date that she was mostly going on because of Farah.

Liar!

Okay, maybe there's more to it, she admitted to herself.

"You doing okay?" Jase asked, as he cocked his head to look at her.

"I'm fine," she rushed to assure him, but knew that she was failing miserably.

"Bonnie, tell me what's wrong. Maybe I can fix it."

She took a deep breath, then blurted out what was bothering her. "I'm worried you're spending too much money. I would have been happy with a hamburger, and I just don't want you to go into debt taking me out on a date."

Bonnie clapped her hand over her mouth and looked at Jase with wide eyes. She could see he was struggling not to laugh.

"I said that, didn't I?"

"Oh yeah, you did. Now I know where Lachlan gets it." He let loose a chuckle.

Bonnie sighed. "Amber knows when and how to keep her mouth shut. She got that from my dad. Lachlan and I are just like my mother. She was a true redhead. Lachlan and I just have red highlights, but it results in the temper and us sometimes running our mouths."

"And their father?"

Bonnie took a deep breath. "I met him at a party when I was a senior in high school. I was the typical dork, straight A's. I never drank or did any drugs. The worst thing I had going for me is not the best judgment in friends. I went to some party that they begged me to go to, then they left without me. Barry ended up talking me into drinking, then took me home. He took me out a couple more times. There was always alcohol involved, but I just thought that's what older kids always did."

"Did he hurt you?"

Bonnie looked up and saw Jase's expression was locked solid. A muscle was twitching along his jaw.

"No, absolutely not. It was all my idea. He told me everybody did it, and I wanted to be like everybody else, so we..." Bonnie looked down at her lap again.

"We did it. I didn't like it. After that, he never called me again."

She took a deep breath and smiled at Jase. "My parents were wonderful. They never sounded or acted the least bit disappointed. When I told Barry I was pregnant, he swore he'd never touched me. My parents went to his parents, but they wouldn't respond. When I went through my parents' papers after they died, I saw dad had hired an attorney to go after him for child support, but then he must have realized the same as me that Barry would have access to the twins. He knew that would not be a good thing, so he dropped it."

Jase reached across the table and gently pried her hand out of the fist she had made and tangled their fingers together. "How long ago did your parents die?"

"They died in a car wreck when the twins were two."

"Were they able to leave you with anything?"

"They left me with the most important thing possible. They left me with a solid bedrock of how to be a parent. But if you mean life insurance or anything like that, no. There were problems with the twins' birth, and the medical bills put them into bankruptcy. By the time they died, there was nothing."

"Aw hell, honey."

"Like I said, it all worked out the way it should have. By the time they died, I'd already had my cosmetology license, because mom took an early retirement so she could stay with my babies. When I lost Mom and Dad, I just couldn't stand the thought of staying in Norfolk, and luckily a friend of mine knew about the opening here in Virginia Beach at the Trinity Salon and I jumped at the chance. Especially when she told me I could rent her house. That was four years ago."

"That's amazing."

"What are you talking about? I'm just one of many single mothers out there. Trust me, there's a whole slew of us." Bonnie grinned. "Now that I've told you my life story, it's only fair that you spill your guts."

"Your dinner will be right out," their server said as he put Jase's beer in front of him.

"Thank you." Jase looked back at Bonnie. "So, you want me to spill my guts, huh?"

"Only seems fair." She gave him a crooked smile.

"You know I can't talk about my work, right?"

"Yep, I get that. But some women who come into the salon are actually wives of SEALs. They have shared some of the funniest stories about the practical jokes that y'all play on one another."

"Well, that's fair game," Jase agreed.

"But I'm interested to know about Renzo, your Brazilian wrist-kissing brother. As well as Malik and Angelica. Farah's mentioned that your mom and dad traveled the world and Malik was adopted here in the States. It all sounds fascinating."

Jase laughed. "I'm not sure fascinating is how I would describe it. I'd describe it as a pain in my ass. Every time I turned around, there was some new brother or sister that Dad was insisting I had to share my shit or my room with. Then he'd tell me it was my job to be a role model. Malik, Renzo, and Bruno were the worst," Jase said with a fond smile.

Every time that dimple of his made an appearance, she thought about licking it.

"Here's your food." Their waiter stood by as an assistant server set down the two sides and a roast-size piece of meat with four slices already cut that looked mouthwatering. This looked better than any prime rib that Bonnie had ever had.

After they loaded up their plates and started eating, Bonnie began asking questions.

"I think you're full of bull-pucky. How could Malik, Renzo, and Bruno be the worst when you're so close to Malik?"

Jase grinned. There was that dimple again. "We were all close in age, size, and athletic ability, so we were always competing with one another. At least we were once we all hit high school. Just when one of us seemed to come out on top, then another one started taking the lead position. Like I said, they were pains in my ass."

Bonnie could hear the fondness in Jase's voice.

"By the way, Renzo is Peruvian, Bruno is Brazilian and Malik was born here in the States. Obviously, he's African American. As for me, no real clue. I look Hispanic, but hell, I could be Brazilian or Peruvian for all we know. Mom and Dad adopted me when I was a few weeks old."

"What about Angelica? I met her at the party, too."

"Angelica?" Jase paused. "We adopted her when she was just a little thing."

"We? You mean your parents, don't you?"

"No, I mean we. Malik, Renzo and me. We adopted

her." Jase paused again. She could see he was in a different time, a different place.

"She was little, huh? Tell me about her. Where did you meet her?"

"She was adopted while we were living in Brazil. She came before Gustavo and Bruno were adopted. She couldn't have been more than two, but it was hard to tell, she hadn't had much food. Malik, Renzo, and I fell in love with her the minute we saw her."

Bonnie didn't ask about Gustavo and Bruno, it was clear that Angelica was the star of this story, and she wanted to hear more. She wanted to hear everything.

"Tell me about her," she prodded.

He looked over at her, then gave a rueful smile. "You sure about that? It's a long story."

"I'm positive."

"Okay, you can't say I didn't warn you. At this point there were only four of us Drakos kids, and we were living and going to school in Curitiba where Dad was overseeing the construction of an airport. He was pulled away for two months to advise on some stadium in Rio de Janeiro. Mom decided to pull us out of school so she could show us all that Rio offered. That included taking the train up Sugarloaf Mountain to see the Christ the Redeemer statue three times."

"Three times, huh?"

"Yep. It never changed, but Mom swore she saw something different in Christ's eyes every time. Dad says it was the Irish in her."

Bonnie gave an incredulous laugh. "My dad used to

say the exact same thing about my mom. Does your mom have red hair too?"

"No, but Grandma Maureen does. She was born in Ireland."

Bonnie smiled. Somehow, hearing how their moms were alike made her feel even more comfortable around him. It was stupid, but there it was.

"Did she homeschool you those two months?"

"You bet your ass she did. Plus, we visited all the churches, museums, missions, and everything else that had any kind of historical significance. Eleni, my older sister, dug in her heels and stayed in Curitiba with one of her friends and continued school there. But the two boys and I were all for missing school. It was one big adventure."

"So, how did you meet Angelica?"

Jase raked his fingers through his hair. It was the first time Bonnie had picked up on any kind of nervous tic from the man. "Mom made friends with ladies at the church we were attending. They were going to go visit an orphanage that was hours out of town. They'd heard they took in kids from Rio's favelas and were doing good work. Mom was interested after some changes that she'd helped to instigate in the orphanages in Peru."

Bonnie had questions, but she didn't interrupt. She was too interested to hear about Angelica.

"So, if Mom went, the three of us had to go. Plus, we had to put on church clothes again. That sucked." Jase gave a small smile as he took another bite of his meat, then washed it down with a sip of his beer. Bonnie watched him swallow.

Even his neck was sexy.

"Anyway, it was some kind of celebration for the orphanage. If you could call it that." Again, Bonnie could see that Jase was lost in his memories, and this time she could see they weren't good.

"What happened when you got there?" she asked.

"Out of the three of us boys, I was the only one who'd picked up Portuguese since we'd arrived. The other two were fluent in English and Spanish, same as me, but they were lagging behind in Portuguese."

"Portuguese?"

"I know, kind of weird. But that's the national language of Brazil. During the ceremony they translated everything into English so Mom could understand. I caught on real quick that they wanted Mom to donate and find other Americans to donate. The little weasel in charge kept droning on. That's when me and the other two decided to go snooping." Jase looked over at her. "Do you like your food?"

Bonnie looked down in surprise and saw that more than half her meal was gone. "I love it. But I enjoy listening to your story even more."

"Okay, but soon you're going to be on the hot seat. I'm going to want to hear all about Bonnie Larkin."

"Yeah, but I already told you everything."

Jase snorted. "I doubt that."

"Keep going. You were at the snooping part."

"Renzo had been in a bad orphanage in Peru. He warned us about what we could find. I didn't believe him." Jase carefully set down his knife and fork on the edge of his plate and dabbed his mouth with his napkin. "Fuck, Bonnie, I just didn't believe him."

Bonnie's mouth went dry.

I'm going to hate this. I know it.

She took a sip of water.

"Malik, Renzo, and I ended up finding where they were housing the sick and incorrigible children in actual cages way in the back of the facility. It was God awful. It was just like Renzo had warned us."

"Cages? Not actual cages. You mean they were locked up separately and... and..."

Jase's jaw was granite.

"Cages, Bonnie. Five fucking cages."

Her eyes began to sting. She prayed God that she could keep her food down.

"The three of us knew we had to do something. Then I saw two young children abusing Angelica. I rescued her."

"What do you mean abusing her?"

Jase lifted his eyebrow and shook his head. "Trust me, you don't want to know. I got her away from them before they could do permanent damage."

I'm going to be sick.

For long moments they both were silent. "Are you okay?" Jase asked.

Bonnie shook her head. Then nodded. "I'm fine. Keep going. I want to know what happened next. How old were you?"

"I was fourteen."

"What happened after you rescued her?"

"A lot happened, but I didn't pay much attention. I went off into a corner and rocked my little angel..."

Bonnie waited for him to continue.

"She was so quiet, Bonnie. She wasn't crying or anything. She was covered in bruises. I started singing a lullaby."

She pictured the big man across from her as a gangly fourteen-year-old, rocking a catatonic baby, singing a lullaby. It about broke her heart.

Jase looked up at her. "She finally reached out to me, Bonnie. She reached out and touched my face. That's the very instant I knew she was going to come home with me."

"And she did," Bonnie whispered.

Jase nodded.

"Renzo and Malik came and saw her. They thought the same thing. Even if Mom fixed things at the orphanage, Angel would come home with us. We were going to adopt her."

"And now she's Angelica." Bonnie gave a wobbly grin.

Jase smiled indulgently. "Yep, that's my girl. She was nominated for a Golden Globe two years ago. Of course, she ends up on the front page of every tabloid, and occasionally needs rescuing because she has shit taste in men. But what are you going to do?" Jase gave a heavy sigh. But despite the bullshit, Bonnie heard the pride in Jase's voice.

"What happened to the other kids? The ones in cages?"

"I asked Mom about that. The weasel ended up in

jail. They couldn't close the orphanage, otherwise where would all the kids go, you know?"

Bonnie nodded.

"They turned the running of the orphanage over to a church. Mom arranged for enough donations so that they could put a clinic on-site. She still gets reports on that orphanage to this day."

"I love your mother," Bonnie grinned.

"We all do."

"Farah told me that there are seventeen children in your family. Are you the oldest?"

"No. Mom and Dad had one natural child. Her name is Eleni. Then they found out they couldn't have any more and started adopting. Eleni is the bomb. She lives in California with her husband and four kids. Every time I have to go to Coronado in Southern California, I try to visit her."

"That's nice. Was she uber protective of y'all?"

"Yeah, but I was the oldest boy, so that meant something."

Bonnie could just imagine Jase at Lachlan's age, trying to wrangle his younger brothers and sisters. He would have been a fierce little boy who took his responsibilities seriously.

"So, we haven't talked about our second date," Jase said with a twinkle in his eye.

"We're not even done with our first one. I have to see if the dessert is any good before I can commit to a second date." Bonnie arched her right eyebrow.

"I always provide good desserts," Jace said, the twinkle gone. Instead, his gaze was full of heat.

I bet you do.

"But before we get to that, let's see what *Tease* has on offer," Jase said.

Then, by some kind of voodoo, their waiter appeared. "Would you like to-go boxes?"

Jase nodded.

"Here are the dessert menus." He handed them to both Bonnie and Jase.

"None of this sharing bullshit about dessert, either. I know how women are. I want the molten lava cake, and I want all of it. So, you have to pick whatever you want, and if you can't finish it, you'll just have to take the rest of it home."

"You're kind of boxing me in."

"Damn right I am," Jase agreed.

"Well, on this, you didn't have to. When I saw the coconut cake with raspberry sauce and Chantilly lace, I was sold. Even better, if I take some of it home, my kids will turn their noses up at it, so it will be mine...all mine." Bonnie rubbed her hands together and gave her best impression of a Bond villain laugh.

Jase threw back his head and laughed. "I like your way of thinking, Bonnie."

When their server came back to box their food, Jase tried to insist that all the leftovers go to her since she had more mouths to eat leftovers.

"Like I told you, their palate is mostly tuned into fish sticks, tater tots, and pizza. I can get them to eat a vegetable if I smother it in enough melted cheese."

"How about a small plate just for you?" Jase persisted.

"Okay," Bonnie finally agreed.

Their waiter put a slice of meat, some potatoes, and asparagus into one box for her, and the rest went into boxes for Jase. Then they placed their dessert and coffee orders.

"You know I'm serious, don't you, Bonnie? I really want to take you and your kids out to the games center, with the batting cages and the putt-putt golf, then out for dinner. Is that something that you would be up for?"

Their desserts were placed in front of them, so Bonnie had a moment to think. "Since the kids already met you, I guess it's okay. As long as we clarify that you're just a family friend, and not someone I'm seeing, that would be fine. I've never really dated, because I don't want men coming over and confusing my kids. I don't want them to get attached to a man and then have them disappear. You know?"

Jase took a moment, then nodded. "That's smart."

"I'm glad you think so. I have a couple of friends who say I'm not modeling a healthy lifestyle for my kids, that includes dating. So, I really appreciate your understanding."

Bonnie dug into her cake and almost moaned at how good it tasted. She wasn't sure that there would be anything she could take home, because she would finish it all here at the restaurant, despite all she'd eaten.

"This weekend wouldn't be good. I have them signed up for two days of camp. They'll be there from ten to six. But next weekend would."

"And after you get home and decide on my score

tonight, perhaps I can take you on another date in the meantime."

"Score?" Bonnie asked.

"Yeah, how well I did on the date. I figure anyone who had the one do-over rule probably scores their dates to determine if they'll go out with the guy again."

Bonnie laughed, then covered her mouth when it came out like a giggle-snort.

Jase smiled. "You're too cute for words."

"Sure I am. Anyway, you're assuming I go out on enough dates to have a scoring system."

"Well, don't you?"

"Don't make me snort again. Are you kidding? When would I have time, and who can I bribe to babysit? Hazard pay is required."

Jase chuckled. "They're just normal kids."

"They convinced one babysitter that I was really an undercover cop, and they weren't really my children. They convinced her that the pizza delivery guy would be our backup, but she had to order almost everything off the menu so he'd know that they were in trouble. When she wouldn't do it, Amber told her if the bad guys found them, and she saw them, then she'd either die or have to go into the witness protection program."

Jase was leaning closer and closer across the table as she told her story. "Is that for real?"

"Yep, it was just three months ago. Amber likes movies like Jason Bourne and the Jack Ryan series. Her first love was *The Professional* with Natalie Portman."

"Those are intense movies for six- and seven-year-olds."

"Tell me about it. Last summer when school was out, I had my neighbor, Mrs. Atwood, watching the kids. A lovely, older lady. She's close to seventy, and too sweet for her own good. She raised one daughter who must have been perfect, because it doesn't even occur to her that my two could ever be lying or wreaking havoc. Lachlan wanted to watch the *Call of Duty* movie and had been complaining to Amber about the parental controls I had put on our cable. My lovely daughter Googled how to get around them."

"Doesn't that require a password?"

"That was totally my fault. Amber heard me tell Mrs. Atwood and a couple of other people what our home alarm code was. She must have memorized it."

Jase nodded. "I've got it. You used the same numeric code for the parental controls."

"Bingo. Jase, I'm telling you, they are little genius criminals and they're only in second grade. You really don't want to take them out."

"The more stories you tell me, the more I want to take them out."

"You're deranged."

5

As Jase's Mustang pulled to a stop at the curb in front of Bonnie's home, he turned to her. "Wait for me to help you out of the car, okay?"

Bonnie nodded.

Jase turned off the car. He prowled over to her side to open the door and assist her out of the car.

"I missed doing this," he muttered.

"What?"

"The valet got to do this at the restaurant."

"I'm going to stick with my original hypothesis. You're a goof."

"But I'm a goof you're willing to put up with. Admit it," he said as they went up her walkway.

"You're right, I admit it," she murmured softly.

Jase struggled to hear the words, but he did.

He watched as she stood in front of her locked door, and he watched as she considered asking him inside. He did nothing to sway her. This was totally up to her. He was really hoping that she would, but there was a part of him that was hoping she wouldn't. He could tell she needed to be wooed.

"Would you like to come in for another cup of coffee?"

He stood on the porch, looking down at her. "I'm not interested in another cup of coffee." He finally replied.

He watched as disappointment flickered across her face before she quickly masked it behind a wall of indifference.

"But, Bonnie, if you're asking me in for a goodnight kiss, I would love to come in."

He watched as she bit her lip. "If I say yes, are you going to expect more than a kiss?" she asked quietly. He looked down and saw her hands trying to strangle her silver clutch.

"I'm going to expect whatever you want to give me. Hell, if you let me inside and give me a peck on the cheek and send me on my merry way, I'm still going to leave here a lucky man. Do you know why?"

She shook her head.

"Because I had one of the best nights of my life, because I got to spend it with you."

He saw her tremble, then push her door wide open. "Jase, I'd like you to come in for the kiss that I've been thinking about since I had my hands in your hair at the shampoo bowl."

He slowly grinned. "In that case, I would love to come in."

Bonnie unlocked her door, then swiftly went inside and pressed the code to unarm the alarm. Jase turned on the hall light and closed the front door, then locked it. She looked over her shoulder at him and smiled shyly.

"Can I take your coat?"

Jase grinned.

"Oh. Yeah. You're not wearing one. Duh." Bonnie shook her head.

"How about you let me help you out of your coat," Jase said as she worked on the knot of her trench coat. When she got it done, he helped her slip it off.

"Closet?" he asked. She pointed to the door close to where they were standing, and he hung it up.

He watched her walk to the living room and turn on all the lamps. The woman wasn't sure about a little snuggling. *Interesting*. Well, she *had* said that she didn't date.

Jase walked to where the hall met the living room and watched her hesitate as she stood in front of her sofa. She was wringing her hands.

"Can you come here, Bonnie? I find myself desperately in need of a hug," he said softly.

"A hug?"

He watched as her expression changed from trepidation to confusion.

"Definitely a hug. Ever since I saw you tonight, I wanted to kiss you, but then we started sharing bits and pieces of our lives, and I got to know you so much better. You're an extraordinary woman, and I need a hug from you. Can you give me one?"

She smiled and walked over to him. "Of course, I can hug you, but I'm not extraordinary. You're the one who's extraordinary. You've spent years serving our country. You're a hero. I'm just a woman who does hair for a living while raising two kids."

As she talked, Jase wrapped one arm around her and took the one step necessary to bring them together, chest to chest. Bonnie was forced to say that last sentence with her head tilted backward so she could look him in the eye.

"We'll have to agree to disagree." He heard his voice lower, almost as if he were talking to a skittish horse. "Put your arms around me, baby. You promised me a hug."

"Oh, yeah."

Jase closed his eyes, reveling in the feel of her embrace. He pulled her even closer with his arm around her waist, then he cupped her cheek as he opened his eyes.

"If you won't agree on extraordinary, will you believe me if I tell you I believe you're beautiful inside and out?"

"No. You don't know me well enough to make that call," she murmured.

"I see I have my work cut out for me. We're going to have to spend a lot of time together so that I can get you to take a compliment." His thumb stroked her bottom lip.

He bent his head slowly until his mouth hovered above hers, their breaths mingling. Bonnie pushed up and met his mouth with hers. Electricity shot through him. It was as if he had just been knocked off his surfboard on the North Shore of Oahu by a twenty-foot wave. He hauled her closer. She mewled into his mouth, and gripped his short hair, her nails sinking into his scalp. Jase returned the favor, tangling his fingers in her hair and tilting her head just a little so that he could get just the right angle for a deeper kiss.

Their tongues met, and she sucked at him. His cock swelled as he thought about her sucking it down. She pulled away for a moment, panting for air, then she was back. Jase nipped at her lush lower lip he had been staring at all night. Bonnie moaned as she pulled his head down closer.

Baby girl liked it when he played a little rough. Jase needed more, and they weren't going to get it standing at the edge of her living room. He easily picked her up and deposited her gently on her comfortable sofa. He braced himself on top of her. He could see the trepidation in her eyes.

"We will stop the moment you want to. We're taking this at your pace," Jase said as he looked down at the beautiful woman beneath him. Her strawberry-gold curls flowed against the blue patterned pillow, and Jase took a moment to slow things down by taking one curl and twirling it around his finger.

He stroked back the fine wisps of her hair that lingered on her cheek.

Bonnie clutched at his shoulders, her nails digging in, but she had a pensive look on her face. Then she bit her lower lip and he saw a blush creep up from her neck to her face.

"Tell me, baby. It's all good."

She wiggled against him and her hips connected

with his erection.

"I'm not having sex with you tonight."

"I knew that before I asked you out," Jase whispered in reply.

"Then why did you ask me out?" Bonnie frowned. "I'm not even sure if you're going to get sex on the third date, like you're supposed to."

Jase laughed.

She was adorable.

"Bonnie, I meant it. We're taking this at your pace. Not just tonight, but all the times we're together, and I intend for us to be together for quite a while."

Bonnie's frown deepened.

"I don't understand you. Why me?"

"Do you like me?" Jase asked. "Do you want to go out on another date with me after putt-putt with your kids?"

Jase found himself holding his breath until she nodded.

"Yes, I want to. I had a wonderful time tonight."

"Well, if you had a wonderful time, why wouldn't I have had a wonderful time? Why wouldn't I want to repeat the experience?"

He watched her closely and saw his argument finally sinking in as her eyelids lowered and she gave him a slow grin.

"I do give good conversation," she purred.

Jase braced all of his weight on his right forearm and cupped her jaw.

"It's more than that. I liked you at Malik's. It was a kick-and-a-half to see you wrangling your two kids. You never lost your temper, and you held them accountable. You reminded me of every outstanding commander I'd ever worked under." At that moment, he realized something else. He'd wanted her before he had ever set eyes on her. All that sass and laughter while she'd been on the phone on the other side of the bushes had entranced him.

Bonnie nuzzled into his hand and kissed his palm. But Jase would not be deterred. "Then there was the fact that I was the typical guy, and I was intrigued because you weren't interested in me."

Bonnie's expression changed, and she rolled her eyes. "You do realize that was not a game. I was not trying to get you to chase after me."

"Which, after I got shit from my family, made me want to chase you all the more."

"And they say it's hard to understand women," Bonnie sighed. "You men can have just as convoluted thinking as we do."

"I never said otherwise." Jase stroked his hand downward so it rounded her throat, his thumb measuring her every heartbeat.

"But I really, really wanted to get to know you. And I mean spend some quality time talking with you, and touching you, as you cut my hair. Jesus, Bonnie, I had to work naming all the capital cities around the world and their leaders, just to keep my dick from bursting out of my jeans during that fucking shampoo."

Her pulse sped up and her eyes dilated. Apparently, he wasn't the only one who'd been turned on by the whole shampoo experience.

"I enjoyed touching you. It turned me on, too," she admitted after a long pause. "You smelled wonderful. I wanted to smell your neck and wrap my arms around you."

"That was the shampoo," Jase protested.

"No, that was before the shampoo," Bonnie assured him. "You turned me on."

"Thank fuck," Jase said with relief. "Then for me, dinner sealed the deal. You're a pleasure to talk to. I like how you can explain your perspective on things, even though we both know you're wrong," he teased.

Bonnie burst out laughing. "Dream on, Buddy."

"You're an absolute pleasure to be around. Plus, my cock is totally in love with your body."

Bonnie grinned. "Even though it has to wait before it gets to come out and play?"

"I'm going to have a long talk with Mr. Happy. He'll eventually understand." Jase said with a grimace that turned into a grin.

"Mr. Happy?" Bonnie giggled.

"At eleven
, I figured out just how happy my penis could make me. He became Mr. Happy."

"Fair enough." Bonnie continued to giggle.

"So, do I get another date after putt-putt?"

"As long as my kids don't hate you," she said as she wrapped her arms around his neck.

"Do you think I might make it to second base tonight?"

"If you're a really good boy, I think it's highly likely," she murmured against his lips.

BONNIE WATCHED as Jase went into the batting cage with Lachlan and showed him how to hold the bat and place his feet so that he would have more control when he swung the bat. He stayed behind Lachlan for five swings, praising him each time he hit the ball, and providing feedback each time he missed. It was the one-on-one training that he had been missing from his little league coach. Marla was just stretched too thin, coaching fifteen seven-year-olds.

After Jase watched Lachlan hit four balls in a row, he went over to the next cage where Amber stood. The machine was pitching softballs to her. Bonnie had been watching her out of the corner of her eye. Her girl had been doing well on her team at catching balls in the field, but she consistently struck out. She prayed Jase could help her with her batting skills. Bonnie moved forward so she could hear what he had to say.

"Amber, your swings are outstanding. I can tell you have the power to make home runs if you connect with the ball."

Amber let the bat fall to the ground, the tip scraping against the rubber mat as she looked up at Jase. "Really?"

"Really," Jase nodded. "But before you can let loose all that power, first you need to learn a couple of secrets. After you learn and practice those, *then* you release your power."

"Are you tricking me?"

Jase knelt down in front of her. "Scout's honor, I'm not tricking you."

"You're a guy. Softball is for girls. How do you know your secrets will work with a softball?"

Jase laughed. "You're as smart as your mama. You take nothing at face value."

"You mean we ask a lot of questions?" Amber asked.

"Yep." Jase nodded. "That's exactly what I mean. Anyway, I've played on a lot of co-ed softball teams, so I know these secrets will work."

Amber's face lit up, and Bonnie could see her daughter's gap-toothed smile.

"Okay, show me."

"Can I ask you a question first?"

Amber nodded.

"When you're up to bat, what usually happens? How many balls, and how many strikes are there?"

"It's usually three strikes and I'm out."

"Is that because you swing at the first three balls?"

Amber nodded.

Jase grinned. "You're a lot like me. I don't have a lot of patience either. I want to swing and get 'er done. Is that what you're thinking?"

Amber grinned. "Exactly. Those girls who just stand there and let the ball pass them by slow down the game."

Jase held out his fist and Amber bumped her fist against it. "I hear you, Amber. But do you ever have to work on an assignment with a partner at school?"

Amber rolled her eyes. "Yes. I got Lori last time."

"Was she helpful?"

"No, she hardly did nothing. I had to do everything. I wanted to tell my teacher, but I don't snitch."

Jase nodded. "So, you understand everybody should do their job well, right?"

"Yeah."

"So don't you think the pitcher on the other team should do a good job?"

Amber sighed. "I thought you were going to tell me secrets. This is boring."

Bonnie fought back a giggle.

That's my girl.

"Stick with me for another two minutes, will you?" Jase asked.

Shit, he's using his puppy dog eyes.

Amber sighed again. "Okay."

"So, if you agree that the pitcher on the other team should do a good job, then she needs to pitch you good balls to hit. And until she does, you shouldn't swing. You deserve good balls to swing at, don't you think?"

"How do I know if it's a good ball?"

Go, Jase! You're getting my daughter to understand!

"Well, this machine only throws strikes. So, you're going to learn to hit these pitches, and learn to hit them well. Then once you do, you'll know if the pitcher from the other team is throwing a good ball to you. Yeah?"

Amber grinned. "Yeah."

"Let's get you hitting some balls."

The next twenty minutes were spent with Jase showing Amber things like not resting her bat on her shoulder. Instead, she needed to have it angled up a little past parallel to the ground. He showed her where her feet should be, and how to shift her weight on her back foot when the ball was thrown.

"I know I told you a lot of things, but the most important is to keep your eye on the pitcher, and then on the ball. Pretend she is Lori, and it's your job to watch how she does her job. Don't look at your bat. Don't look at your feet. Just relax and watch Lori, then watch the ball as it comes to you."

Jase stepped back. Amber took a soft swing and the ball popped off her bat.

"Perfect!" Jase yelled. "You did that exactly right. Now let's do it again."

"But it didn't go far," Amber complained.

"What were we trying for? A home run, or you connecting with the ball?" Jase teased.

Amber laughed. "You're right. That was my first hit since T-ball."

"Okay, let's do 'er again."

Bonnie watched her daughter hit ball after ball. Even Lachlan came out of his batting cage so he could watch his sister. "Go Amber," he yelled.

Bonnie didn't think she'd ever grinned so widely.

I'm going to give Jase free haircuts for life!

JASE LOOKED at the two kids in the back of his crew cab. They were passed out. When he looked over at Bonnie in the passenger seat, he realized she could use some sleep as well.

"How many hours a week do you work?" Jase asked quietly.

"Not too much," Bonnie said.

Which meant she worked too much.

"How many is not too much? Can you quantify that?"

"When I'm solidly booked, probably sixty hours a week. A slow week is forty-five hours a week. After the kids started going to school all day, I started taking on more clients. I'd been saving for the house, so I had the down payment ready, but not the income level. After I took on the additional clients I qualified, so I became a homeowner," she grinned.

"That's fantastic."

"Thank you."

Jase could hear the bone-deep satisfaction in her voice. And she should be satisfied. He didn't know many people, men or women, who could have twins at such a young age without her mom and dad to lean on, and no kind of help from the baby daddy or his parents and still make a success out of their life.

"I told you about my menagerie of a family. What about you? Any aunts, uncles, cousins?"

"My parents were both only children. I always dreamed about having a..." She trailed off.

"What? What'd you dream about?"

"Nothing. I'm just overtired." He heard her fake a yawn as he pulled up in front of her house. He let it slide. After all, this was only the fourth time they'd been in one another's presence, even though he felt like he'd known her a lot longer than that.

He pulled into the parking space in front of her house and turned off his truck, then looked over his shoulder at the two children. They'd been zonked out since two minutes after leaving the restaurant.

Bonnie pushed at her door.

"Baby, let me," Jase whispered.

"Huh?"

"Open your door for you."

This woke her up. Her eyes twinkled. "You're kidding, right? I mean, opening the door at the restaurant is one thing, but coming around and opening my car door when I don't have a broken arm is kind of a bit much, don't you think?"

"It's how I was raised. It means a lot to me to do this kind of thing for a woman I respect."

She gave him her crooked smile with a flustered gaze. "All right," she whispered. Jase could tell he had taken her by surprise.

Good. Maybe I'm getting through to her. I really didn't want to go buy a hammer and chisel.

Jase hustled out of his truck. He opened her door and helped her step onto the running board, then onto the curb.

"How do you normally do this?" Jase asked. "Do you wake them up? I mean, you're too little to be carrying one of them, even Amber. Do you just normally wake them up?"

"I wake up Lachlan. He's almost eight pounds heavier than Amber, and I feel every pound when I carry him. Amber, I carry."

"You really shouldn't," he admonished as he opened

the back door to his crew cab. It was on the side where Lachlan was sitting on a backless booster.

"I tell you what. I'll carry them both in. You just open the door and handle the alarm. Then point me to their rooms."

Jase forced back a laugh as Bonnie inspected him to see if he would be capable of carrying both of her children at the same time.

"I promise. I'm up for the job."

"Okay, let me hand Amber to you. I don't want you leaning into the truck while you're holding Lach."

"Okay, baby. Whatever eases your mind." He bent into the back and unclipped Lachlan, then picked up the little boy.

"What?" Lachlan's voice was slurred with sleep.

"It's all good, Tiger. We're home." Jase assured him.

"S'kay." His eyes closed, and he snuggled against Jace's chest. Again, Jase had to force down a laugh as he saw Mama Bear watching the entire interaction as if Jase were disarming a bomb. He tilted his head. Bonnie nodded.

Jase started around the front of the truck and Bonnie had Amber's door open by the time he got to her.

He got an arch look. Apparently, he wasn't supposed to open the door. He shook his head in resignation, then smiled. He watched as Bonnie reached in and pushed her daughter's curly hair off her face, then kissed her forehead as she unbuckled her belt and picked her up.

"Mom?" Amber asked.

"Right here, sweetheart," Bonnie whispered as she stood up beside the truck.

"Can I hit more balls?"

"Time to sleep first."

"S'kay."

"Is it okay if Jase carries you inside?"

"S'kay."

Amber leaned over to Jase. He easily caught her up in his right arm. She slid her legs and arms around him like a little monkey.

"Can I hit more balls tomorrow?"

"No, honey, not tomorrow." Bonnie said.

"Jase, will you take me to hit balls tomorrow?"

"Nope. Right now, you have to go to bed like your momma said," Jase whispered.

"Fine. If I have too." Then she rested her head on his shoulder, and immediately fell back to sleep.

Jase forced back a laugh.

Bonnie smiled at him as she saw that both of her children were sound asleep in his arms. "Lead the way," he smiled back at her.

Bonnie made it up the walkway to her front door and Jase easily kept up with her. He watched as somehow, she put her hand in her huge purse and came out with her keys in seconds. She unlocked the door and stepped back so he could go in first.

She closed and locked the door, then reset the alarm.

"This way," she whispered.

He followed her down the short hallway. She pushed open a door that led into a room that was painted with soft green walls and had Wonder Woman and Einstein posters up on the walls. Jase was loving this girl more and more. Bonnie motioned for Jase to place her on the yellow-flowered bedspread.

"I'll get her dressed for bed after I show you where to put Lachlan."

His bedroom was down the hall.

No posters for this kid, but he seemed to have every single action figure for Iron Man known to mankind. Each one was lovingly displayed on shelves near his bed. He even had an Iron Man bedspread. Looked like Mama indulged her boy. Come to think of it, there had been a high-end telescope in Amber's room.

Jase would bet his bottom dollar that Bonnie didn't indulge herself nearly as much as she did her kids.

"I don't want to go to bed," Lachlan said, as Jase laid him down. Then he rolled over, grabbed his pillow, and started to softly snore.

"They've got one-track minds," he chuckled quietly.

"I know," Bonnie said as she headed out of Lachlan's room. "I don't know where they get it from."

Jase snorted. "Yeah, I can't imagine."

"Can I get you something to drink? I have sweet tea, water, soda, lemonade, and I also bought some Dorothy's lager."

Jase stopped as she continued on into the kitchen. She'd remembered and bought the beer he'd ordered at the restaurant? Hell, he could count on three fingers the women who'd done that for him, and none of them had done that after just one date.

She wasn't even trying to impress him; she was just made to observe people, then do nice things for them.

Mom would love her.

"Jase? I'll totally understand if you don't want to stay."

Shit. He hadn't responded.

"I would love the lager," he answered.

She grinned.

That smile lit up her face. Every one of her smiles hit him in the gut. What was it about this woman?

She pulled the bottle out of the refrigerator. "I don't have any beer glasses, but I could pour it into a tall water glass if you'd like."

"The bottle's fine."

"Here you go." She handed him the bottle. "I'm going to get them dressed for bed. I shouldn't be too long."

"I want to know if Amber brings up the batting cages again."

"Oh, she will." Bonnie shook her head and looked heavenward. "That girl."

Jase sat down on the couch. Bonnie fished out the remote from between the cushions. "Here, watch whatever you want."

"Thanks."

She had a sexy sway even when she was wearing tennis shoes.

Shit, when did I become an ass man? I always thought it was all about a woman's legs. Then again, I'm basically all about Bonnie.

Jase turned on two of the lamps in the living room.

He took his time drinking his beer while he looked around. It might be neat and clean, but there were still plenty of examples of kids living here. He chuckled when he saw three controllers for the PlayStation. Looked like Mom played with her kids. That was great to see. He went to the shelves and saw some battered paperbacks interspersed with a lot of pictures of the twins. Occasionally there would be a picture with the three of them, but mostly it was Bonnie taking pictures of her kids.

Jase picked up one where they were at Disney World. All three of them were sporting Mickey Mouse ears. The kids looked to be about three as they grinned into the camera. Even back then, he could see the mischief in the kids' eyes and the love and pride in Bonnie's. Nothing had changed.

"That's one of my favorites," Bonnie said as she walked into the living room.

"Were they three or four?"

"That was for their fourth birthday. That was the first day when they realized there were some rides they were too small for. After that it was touch and go." Bonnie came to stand next to Jase and he put his arm around her shoulders.

"I like your kids. I liked them at Farah and Malik's house, but I really enjoyed spending time with them today."

"They liked you too. You're now Lach's hero for teaching him how to hit the ball better. My guess is that Amber is still withholding judgment until she sees her hitting the ball at the cages isn't just a onetime fluke."

Jase joined Bonnie's laugh.

"Your daughter is a lot like you. Both of you are hard nuts to crack."

"You aced it with the food. They loved the macaroni and cheese, meatballs, and the spumoni. Lachlan was so relieved to see it was ice cream." They both laughed. "My daughter can also be bought with good food."

Jase put down the picture and turned Bonnie in his arms so they were looking at one another. "I know you don't want to introduce a boyfriend to your kids." Jase winced at the word.

"I don't know how anybody could call you a boy," Bonnie said as she looked up at him. "But you're right, I never want my kids to get caught up in mommy having men friends or boyfriends hanging around and then disappearing. I refuse to do that to my children."

"I respect that. I like how I'm just Malik's brother. But is it safe for Malik's brother to kiss you?" Jase asked. He glanced toward the twins' bedrooms.

"I could call my kids' names with a bullhorn and it wouldn't wake them, not after the day they had."

"In that case." Jase touched his lips to hers, and she sighed with pleasure.

AND SHE'D THOUGHT the other night's kiss was potent. Boy, was she wrong. Tonight's kiss was out of this world. Maybe it had something to do with how he had interacted with her babies. Bonnie wasn't sure. But right now, here in the safety of Jase's arms, she was melting.

Jase feathered his fingers against her jaw and it caused tingles to cascade through her entire body. He must have felt her shivers because he pulled her closer. He held her up. Her fingers twisted into the sides of his t-shirt, trying to find purchase in a world that was swirling around her.

Tonight, Jase's kiss wasn't slow and seductive like before. Instead, he was hungry and greedy, and Bonnie reveled in it. That she caused this big, experienced man to feel this way about her made her feel beautiful and desired.

Then her world felt upside down, and she realized he had picked her up, and before she even realized she was in his arms, he was lowering her to the sofa. Instead of lying over her like he had before, he nestled her against the back of the couch and lay beside her, then tugged the blanket from the top of the couch over them.

Oh goodie. Even if we're at second base, the kids won't be able to tell if they wake up for a glass of water. What a smart man.

"What has you grinning, gorgeous?"

"Just appreciating your attention to detail, that's all." Bonnie tugged at his t-shirt so that she could get her hands on those abs that she had been admiring since the day of the party.

So good. So, so, good.

"So, you plan to make it to second base this time, huh?" Jase asked.

"Seems only fair," Bonnie giggled.

"Let's see if I can distract you."

He put a finger under her chin and her mouth blossomed under his kiss. Soon lips, teeth, and tongues meshed together, both of them trying to get closer. Trying to consume one another.

It was Jase who pulled away first, his breathing heavy. His eyes were glittering wildly. "Too much?"

Bonnie sank her nails into his chest. "Not enough," she breathed.

He dipped his head again, once more overwhelming her with his passion. With his desire. Somehow, Bonnie realized that her flannel overshirt was unbuttoned and now Jase's big hand was pulling her tank top out of the waistband of her Bermuda shorts. She moaned when she felt his hand skate across the hot skin of her stomach, inching ever upwards until he found the front fastening of her bra.

She was grateful when he didn't ask her for permission again. For once, she didn't want to control every aspect of her life. She wanted to give control over to someone else who she trusted. Then she felt the rough warmth of his palm cupping her breast and she shuddered before she pushed up against him.

"You like that," he murmured.

She couldn't get any words out, so she nodded.

He snuck his other hand under her top, and soon both of his hands held her. She twisted and turned as he kneaded her flesh, tugging at her taut nipples. Then his mouth was there, sucking the tip of her breast like she was some kind of tasty candy. He went from one to the other and then back again. With each pass, he suckled harder until finally he scraped her with his teeth and she let out a soft wail.

Jase immediately covered her mouth with his, blocking out any other sound she might have made, but that just meant his hands pressed tighter against her needy flesh. Bonnie could hear herself groan deep in her throat as one of his hands continued to caress her, and another journeyed south.

When Jase circled her belly button, she arched against him, wishing he was on top of her, not beside her. As if he read her mind, he rolled her underneath him and his potent erection pressed against her core.

She broke their kiss so she could breathe. "We need to go to my bedroom."

"No." Jase kissed her temple. "We're not leaving this couch. Trust me, gorgeous. Everything will be fine."

His eyes shone like black diamonds. Finally, she nodded her head. He gave her a slow, smiling kiss. Then his hand trailed even further south until he came to the button of her shorts. Bonnie sucked in her stomach. Whether to make it easier for him to unbutton her shorts or to tuck in her tummy, she wasn't sure.

In moments her zipper was down and she trembled as she felt Jase's hand cup her core.

"Drenched," he murmured.

Before she could get embarrassed, he bit her earlobe. "Finding you this wet for me makes me feel ten feet tall," he whispered in her ear.

Bonnie relaxed her legs and Jase took full

advantage. One of his fingers stroked along the seam of her pussy until he coaxed her clitoris out of hiding. She jerked as lightning shot through her.

He was relentless. He circled and stroked her for what felt like hours, but were probably only long minutes. Bonnie found herself mewling for more.

"Shhh, you need to be quiet, baby. I'll take care of you, but you need to be quiet."

Bonnie thought about moving her hand out from under his shirt, but she didn't have the will or the coordination. Still, she persisted. She moved her right hand down Jase's side until she reached his belt.

"No, Bonnie. Not tonight. Tonight is all about you. Put your hand back where it was. I like the feel of your hands on my chest."

As soon as he said that, he parted the lips of her sex and pushed two fingers inside her. Bonnie whimpered.

Jase lifted his head, watching her carefully. "Too much?"

She shook her head, hair flying. It would have been if he hadn't prepared her. She let out a low whine.

"Bonnie?"

"More," she said as she arched up, greedily forcing a deeper penetration.

He gave her that smile she adored, the one where his dimple popped.

Each time he thrust in; his thumb brushed across her clit.

"You feel so good, baby. Give me more. I want to bathe in your excitement."

Embarrassed, Bonnie slammed her face into the crook of his neck.

"No, gorgeous. Don't turn away from me." Again, he tipped her head so that her eyes were on him. "Do you know how good it feels to have your channel clench my fingers? Your pussy weep with excitement?"

She shook her head.

"The only thing better than this will be watching you come." He drove deeper and faster. His thumb circled her clit.

It was too much, but not enough, and somehow Jase knew it. He increased the pressure and found a place inside her body that had her slanting up even higher. Her entire body clenched, then trembled. She was out of control. He dragged his fingers against that magical spot, then flicked her clit and a tidal wave of ecstasy transported her out of her body, up into the stars. As she opened her mouth to cry out, his lips slammed down on hers, swallowing down her shriek.

Long, long moments—minutes? —later, Bonnie found herself buttoned up, her head resting against Jase's chest, his heartbeat supplying her with a beautiful sense of peace. Then she noticed the hard press of his erection under her hip.

"Jase," she pushed up from his chest. "I haven't done anything for you."

"Yes, you have, baby. Seeing you lost in pleasure was a gift."

"But I can feel your erection. Let me do something for you."

"I've been hard damn near every time I've been

around you, but I've been able to keep it in my pants. That doesn't mean I don't want us to make love, because I do. I just don't want to do it on your couch, always listening to see if your kids might wake up for a glass of water. No baby—when we first make love, it will be when I have the entire night to touch and taste you properly."

Bonnie shivered, and Jase laughed.

"You like the sound of that, don't you?"

She could only nod.

"Now, before one of the kiddos does get up, I think it's time for me to leave. Do you need me to carry you to bed and read you a bedtime story?" His eyebrow arched and his dimple popped as he grinned.

"I don't think that will be necessary."

"Such a shame."

He dipped his head and kissed her.

"Good night, Bonnie," he said as he pushed up from the couch. "Now come walk me to the door and lock up, then don't forget to set the alarm."

Bonnie rolled her eyes as she got up off the couch. "You know, I survived just fine before you came into my life."

"Yeah, but I bet it wasn't nearly as fun."

Again, she rolled her eyes.

Jase dipped down for another slow kiss and Bonnie considered just how close her bedroom was to her front door.

"Nope. No sex tonight," he laughed as he broke off the kiss. "Sweet dreams, gorgeous."

"Nothing but," she promised.

6

On his way to Bonnie's house, Jase's car's Bluetooth read him a message:

"Kostya Barona said, 'Lock things up and come to base, it's time to leave.'"

"You've got to be fucking kidding me!" Jase said as he pounded his Mustang's steering wheel. There wasn't a place to park in front of her house, so he found a spot four houses down. He parallel parked and shot out of his car.

How in the fuck am I going to explain this?

Before he had a chance to knock on the door, Bonnie opened it.

Jase felt something melt inside of him. That was Bonnie, no subterfuge. Once she decided she liked him, cared about him, she wasn't afraid to show it.

Damn, there was a fuck of a lot to lov—like—about this woman.

"You're early." She grinned. "How did I guess that

would happen? Come inside. I'm almost done getting ready. Just gotta decide on which boots to wear."

She was down the hall before he had a chance to talk to her, or even kiss her for that matter. When she came back, she was wearing leather boots that molded to her lower leg perfectly. She was wearing the pumpkin sweater dress he remembered seeing when he'd taken her out for seafood the previous weekend. Come to think of it, he'd noticed repeats in her clothes, but she almost always had different shoes on.

She twisted around to pick up a Lego, giving him a nice side view of Bonnie, and all thoughts of her wardrobe left his head.

Curves. I love women with curves.

He spotted her small suitcase.

"I tell you, one of these days I'm going to kill myself on one of Lachlan's Legos."

"Bonnie—" Jase started, and her head shot up, her gaze penetrating.

"What's wrong?"

"How do you know something's wrong?"

"Call it a mom's intuition. Spill it, Drakos."

"My team has been called to base."

She took a deep breath. "This isn't a drill, is it?"

"Nope."

"When do you have to be there?"

"As long as it takes to get to my house, change my clothes, grab my go-bag and drive my truck to base."

"And you don't know how long you'll be gone, do you?"

He shook his head as he continued to stare at her.

She nodded. "Okay. I know this is part of the drill. The timing sucks, but I'm sure there are other members of your team who are in more delicate situations who think it sucks even more." She gave him her crooked smile.

Adorable.

Jase opened his arms. "Come here. I need a kiss."

"Yippee, since the kids aren't here, I get tongue action!" Bonnie grinned as she practically danced over to him and wound her arms around his neck.

Yeah, leaving her is going to kill.

"Bloody hell, fuck!"

Shit, Mateo almost sounded like his brother Renzo when he swore.

"Are you fucking kidding me?" Jonas Wulff yelled.

Another shot hit the Mercedes G-Wagen. They were pinned down. "Who are these jokers? And just how many are there?" Jase shouted out his question to any of his team who might know the answer.

"I think it's just one sniper and one man with an assault rifle," Tanner Robb answered Jase. He needed to yell above the din of gunfire.

There were too many civilians. Why in the hell would they be firing at them in such a crowded area? It didn't make sense. This was the reason they'd asked for a public meet, for fuck's sake.

"I've got a bead on the guy with the AK," Tanner said. He was now beneath the Mercedes.

Fuck, the shot's going to have to be perfect not to hit an innocent. Why in the hell are so many people still in the line of fire? Why haven't they hit the concrete or run away? Don't they have any sense of self-preservation?

"Too damn many civilians." Jase heard the disgust in his man's mouth. Tanner was one of the best snipers on the Omega Sky team and being stuck with just a pistol had to be maddening. But Jase trusted him with his life.

"Take the shot," Jase yelled.

"The sniper is shooting from that parking structure across the street!" Mateo yelled.

"Where? Which one?"

Mateo pointed to one of the many parking complexes attached to the Mall of the Emirates. Dammit, Jase had specifically picked this crowded spot for the meet to avoid this kind of shitshow.

Fucking Kraken!

"Got him," Tanner said as he crawled back from under the G-Wagen. "What have we got?"

"A sniper too far away for us to shoot," Mateo said succinctly.

"I'm a decoy. The rest of you scramble. I want him taken out before one more civilian is shot. Got it?"

Jase heard three affirmatives and watched as Mateo, Jonas, and Tanner took off in three different directions. They all crouched low, zigzagging. Thank God Gideon had dressed them up in high-end clothes, so they blended in with the people here near this expensive part of Dubai. With a sniper shooting into the crowd, nobody would question them running, either.

Another shot plowed into the Mercedes. Good, that meant it hadn't hit a civilian, and he was still the target. Jase grabbed the handle to open the passenger side door, but he couldn't. It had been too much to hope that somebody would have left their vehicle unlocked. Jase shot out the passenger window of the vehicle.

"What are you doing?" A man shouted at Jase in Arabic. The young man turned around and motioned to two other teenagers. "He's got a gun."

"I sure do," Jase responded in their language. "But I'm not shooting at anybody but that asshole up there who has killed those people on the sidewalk. I'm the good guy." Jase pointed across the street.

"What are you doing?" One of the new teens demanded to know.

Jase ignored him and unlocked the passenger door from the inside. Then he climbed into the G-Wagen. One of the stupid assholes got hold of his ankle and pulled.

I don't have time for this shit!

Jase turned and pointed the gun at him.

"Let me loose or I'll shoot you instead of the murderer up there."

All three of the teens took a step back. Then the first one stepped up again, and Jase held up his gun. "Back off and wait for the police."

"I hear the sirens," one of the other young men said.

"Good. Let them capture me. In the meantime, leave me the fuck alone!" Jase turned away from them and crawled into the driver's seat, then attempted to roll down the window.

No luck.

He only had one bullet left in his gun and one back-up magazine, but he didn't have any choice. He had to shoot out the window.

He leaned back, turned his head, and shot. Once again, the hole went through the driver's-side window and he had to pull the glass out so that he had room enough to maneuver.

Thud.

The sniper's bullet hit the dashboard.

Fuck, that was close.

Jase scrambled over into the backseat where he didn't have the steering wheel blocking him. Another shot hit the passenger headrest.

One of my men better be over in that parking garage by now.

Why the hell Kostya put him in charge of this part of the overall operation, he wasn't sure. But right now, he sure as hell wasn't happy about it.

Jase pushed out his empty magazine and shoved in the new one. Decision time. Blow out another window, or just let the sniper continue to occupy his time aiming for the front seat?

Thud.

This time the shot hit the glove box and left a fist-sized hole. The guy was using some serious ammo. He definitely wasn't fucking around.

Jase looked up at the parking structure. The guy had to be at the south end, based on the trajectory of the shots. He pulled out his phone and sent Mateo,

Tanner, and Jonas a quick text, letting them know what he'd figured out.

What he wouldn't give for a normal SEAL comm system.

Suddenly Jase heard three consecutive shots ring out. Then he heard a woman scream, then a man.

Dammit! The asshole is shooting at the civilians again!

What purpose did the Kraken have to be trying to kill a potential client? Had they figured out that it was really Omega Sky they were meeting? If so, how?

Maybe I should quit thinking about this shit and pay attention to what's going on around me!

Jase shot out the backseat window. He flew over the car door's window frame toward the parking garage. He knew there was no chance that his bullet would reach that far, but hopefully, it would bring the sniper's attention back to him.

One of the sniper's shots obliterated the steering wheel. Jase heard another shot, but it didn't hit the vehicle he was in. He took another shot up at the parking garage.

"Aim at me, you motherfucker. Aim at *me*."

Jase's phone vibrated.

It was Jonas.

He swiped to answer it.

"Mateo took care of him. Hightail it out of there before the police arrive."

Jase wasted no time. He shoved his gun and phone into his pocket and tried to open the door. It wouldn't work.

Goddammit! Backseat child lock!

He started to climb over the seat to the front.

"Officer, one of them is in there."

Damned teenagers, weren't they supposed to be playing video games?

He heard them coming toward the passenger side of the G-Wagen. Jase stopped climbing. He reached over the seat and unlocked the back door. He shoved it open and ducked low, walking slowly until he reached a crowd of people who were standing around, trying to help the injured, but basically retelling their stories to one another. It was the perfect group to blend in with.

7

Thank God for Gideon Smith, Jase thought for the millionth time. Once again, he'd come through with the best possible accommodations. It sure beat where they had been staying.

"Since you're supposedly hotshot American business executives, you need to look like, smell like, sound like, and room like, hotshot American businessmen," he'd said over the phone this morning.

Jase had understood the clothes, but these connecting kick-ass suites at the Armani Hotel in the world's tallest skyscraper? It was beyond his comprehension.

"Pretty sweet, huh?" Tanner said as he walked into the living room with a towel around his waist. "I could get used to this."

"How much do you think this whole thing costs?" Jase asked.

"I checked it out. One night here covers three mortgage payments for me," Mateo answered from where he was sitting on a leather couch in front of a huge ass flat-screen TV. "For the connecting suites? That means one night pays for half my year of mortgage payments on my condo." Mateo shook his head in disbelief. "Jase, this ain't right."

"You look like hell," Tanner said to Jase. "You might want to go take a shower, then let us know what happened after we left you. We got your text, but we want to know the full story."

"Where's Jonas?" Jase asked.

"He said he had to meet a guy."

Jase looked down at the slim watch that Gideon had given him and the others to wear. He much preferred his bulkier Luminox watch that could withstand a tidal wave and an earthquake as opposed to this thin, fancy, piece-of-shit watch. But at least it told time.

"We meet up with the others at nineteen hundred hours. Jonas better be done scrounging by then. Which room am I bunking in?" Jase asked.

"We put your stuff in the one with Jonas." Tanner pointed to the door that led to the connecting room.

"Jase, isn't the Lieutenant going to lose his mind when he sees where we're staying? I mean, the Navy's per diem usually means we're eating Clif Bars most days."

Tanner laughed and Mateo rounded on him. "What in the hell is so funny? This is a legitimate question. I know Gideon has money. Real money. But don't tell me he's paying for this out of his own pocket."

"You're right, Mateo, he isn't," Jase chuckled. "Gideon enjoys pulling shit like this. I heard about the first time that he did this to the lieutenant. Kostya about lost his damned mind. He was thinking the same thing. How in the hell was he going to justify the cost of some five-star hotel to Captain Hale and accounting?"

"Gideon did it to Kostya?" Mateo didn't sound like he believed him.

"He did. But the thing is, with Gideon involved there is always some kind of mistake in the hotel's billing department, and the final bill always shows for the cheapest room possible with some kind of discount code applied that makes it just under the Navy's per diem amount. That man is slick with computers. If you're ever dating a woman and want him to check her out, he can do one hell of a deep dive for you." Jase looked over at Tanner. "You too, Tanner."

"Thanks, no. Not to say I've always chosen wisely in the past, but I prefer the old-fashioned way of dating. We get to know one another by talking and lying to one another."

Mateo burst out laughing. "That's a good one."

Jase thought about Bonnie and smiled. Damn, it was good to be dating someone who was so forthright. She was definitely a *'what you see is what you get'* kind of woman, and he admired the hell out of her.

"Hey, Jase, before you grab your shower, pick up the phone and ask for something. The service around here is incredible," Tanner said.

"What are you talking about?"

"This place comes with twenty-four-seven service. Just pick up the phone and ask for something. Anything."

Jase rolled his eyes and went to the room phone and picked it up. He didn't even have to press a button. Somebody immediately started speaking English to him.

"Hello. With whom do I have the pleasure of speaking?"

"This is Jase Drakos. What's your name?"

"I am Saeed al Zarooni. I will be at your service for your stay here at the Armani Hotel. How may I assist you?"

"Uhm. Can I get a Pabst Blue Ribbon beer?"

"It would be my pleasure to bring you one. Would you like me to bring you more than one so that you have additional beers stocked in your refrigerator?" Saeed asked.

Jase looked at the phone in his hand. This couldn't be right. Hell, most times in Virginia, he was shit out of luck when he asked for a PBR.

"That would be great, sir."

"Saeed, sir. My name is Saeed."

"In that case, I'm Jase."

"Very good. I will be up with your beer shortly. Would you like me to come to Mr. Robb's and Mr. Aranda's room, or should I bring it to yours and Mr. Wulff's room?"

"Bring it to my room."

"Very good, sir."

"Jase," he reminded the man with a smile.

"Very good, Jase," he said. "I will be there shortly."

Damn. Tanner hadn't been kidding.

Kostya and the men he'd been working with arrived just before nineteen hundred hours. Jase's lieutenant just rolled his eyes when he looked around and saw their accommodations.

"How come you guys got to check out of the Motel 3?" Landon Kelly practically whined. "Shit, I refuse to even walk on the carpet in my bare feet, because I know I'll to end up with some sort of STD if I do."

"Do I need to explain the birds and the bees to you again?" Jase asked as they all chuckled. Landon flipped him the bird.

Gideon was walking in with Ryker following him. "I heard that. Trust me, you have nothing to complain about, you pussy," he said to Landon.

"He's right," Kostya chimed in. "Right now, we're supposed to be trying to hire on with the Kraken. They wouldn't expect down-on-their-luck mercenaries to be staying at the Burj Khalifa."

"I guess not," Landon sighed.

"Jase, I got the picture that you sent to me," Gideon said. "I sent it to Kane MacNamara, and he was able to identify the man. His name was Edward Arden. He spent four years in Leavenworth, then disappeared off the face of the Earth. So how did you get his photo, Jase?"

"Tanner shot him outside of the Mall of the Emirates. Needless to say, our idea of meeting with a member or members of the Kraken in a well-populated area didn't pan out so well."

"Damn," Nolan said quietly. Jase could hear the pain in the man's voice. "I saw that on my Al Jazeera news feed this afternoon. They said that eight civilians were killed in that gunfight. Dozens more were injured. What in the hell happened?"

"It was a set-up. Just a straight-up set-up. You know we got the meet because of Aiden O'Malley's uncle. Aiden is a SEAL in Coronado, and his family has a wide variety of men and women who have extensive friends and contacts. His uncle was able to set it up so that they would meet with us. He explained we were potential clients. Should have been straightforward. Unfortunately, no."

"There was talk of multiple shooters. Was it just this guy and y'all?" Ryker asked.

"Nope. There was a sniper across the street," Jonah answered. "Jase stayed behind as a decoy, hoping to divert his attention away from the civilians. The three of us scrambled and Mateo took him out."

"So, none of you were identified?" Kostya asked.

"Nope," Jase answered. "I was the last one left behind, and I made it out of there, despite the police asking for papers from everyone."

"How'd you manage that?" Gideon wanted to know.

"There was an elderly woman who was injured and alone. I made a big fuss taking care of her, and waving away the police, waiting for an ambulance. When the ambulance came, I bolted."

"Was she all right?" Nolan asked.

"Yeah, she's going to make it. I called her son for

Her Defiant Warrior | 143

her; he and the rest of the family were going to meet her at the hospital."

God, I'm just as sappy as Nolan!

"I want to go over everything again." Kostya said. "I think we might be missing something."

That was never a good sign. If their lieutenant, Kostya Barona, thought they were missing something, you could be damned sure they were missing something.

"Gideon, do you have the video of the briefing with Captain Hale and the CIA Director?"

"If you give me my tablet, I do," he said to Kostya.

"Have you been going through withdrawals?" Kostya asked as he handed over the tablet to Gideon.

"It's not just the computer I'm missing, that's for damn sure." He turned to Jase. "Do you know what the wi-fi code is here?"

Jase shook his head. Then Tanner provided it.

"Give me a minute, and I'll pull up the briefing," Gideon promised, then turned on the television and began tapping some keys on his tablet. While they waited, Jase thought back to when they first arrived in Dubai four days ago.

One of the first things that they'd needed to do was get weapons. Kostya had waited twelve hours for their CIA contact to come through with a way to get weapons in Dubai. When that didn't work out, he assigned Jonas Wulff to take care of it.

Jonas was their guy who was always able to 'find a guy.' This assignment had been no exception. Besides putting in an order for top-of-the-line weapons, Jonas had also asked if his contact had other Americans recently purchasing automatic rifles, sniper rifles and pistols. Unfortunately, his contact wasn't willing to cough up any information that might lead them to the Kraken, but Jonas's contact did mention that there had been a big black market purchase by Danmey Properties. Two weeks ago, the weapons dealer had been asked to deliver one hundred and fifty kilos of C-4 to International City, which is where Danmey's labor camp was located. Jonas put in his order for the weapons their team would need and immediately came back and told the Omega Sky team about the big purchase of explosives.

Kostya had then tasked Gideon and Ryker McQueen to track down the C-4, which led them to the Danmey's construction labor camp in International City. In the last four days, Ryker McQueen had become one of the bosses of the labor camps, and Gideon was posing as one of the day laborers.

"I've got the footage," Gideon said, interrupting Jase's ruminations. "Where do you want me to start this?" he asked Kostya.

"Skip the introductions and start at the part where the Director of the CIA was explaining to Captain Hale what he had discovered and what he wanted us to do."

It took a moment, but soon the hotel's large flat screen television was filled with Director Howard of the CIA and their captain, Josiah Hale. It wasn't obvious to the casual observer how pissed the Director was, but if you were looking for it, you could tell he was furious.

"One of the members of my support team hired the

Kraken Elite to take out the US Consular General and her top aids in Dubai," the director began. "In order to divert suspicion of this hit, this little pissant paid the Kraken to also take out the British Embassy in Dubai as well. They were supposed to get this done within thirty days of being hired. Now we have nineteen days left, so it could happen today or nineteen days from now." The director continued. "Normally I would just have the US Consulate and the British Embassy shut down, but there's going to be members of the United Nations coming to Dubai this month and our consulate needs to remain open."

"And the British Embassy?" Captain Hale asked.

"Same situation. They can't postpone the UN visit. We have brought in Britain's MI6. Both buildings have doubled their security. Our Marines and the UK Royal Marines have both been put on notice. We're not sure how many men the Kraken have now. We know they have been actively recruiting since the death of Frank Sykes. It is my understanding that they are now recruiting internationally."

"Who's in charge now?" Ryker McQueen asked. Ryker was the man who had killed Frank Sykes, the previous leader of the Kraken.

"We know Ely Roberts is now the leader and Ephram Brady is now his lieutenant. According to the man we have in custody, all of his communication was through Ephram. Our sources are telling us there is now another lieutenant out of Australia. That's all we know at the moment."

"So, you don't know how many men on the Kraken

team might be trying to take down the embassies?" Kostya asked.

"No. But I know our guy put out a fifteen-million-dollar contract. Half up front. That should have paid for a lot of personnel."

"How did he get his hands on so much money?" the captain asked the director.

"That's part of the reason he wants the US Consular General dead. She was close to finding out what he was doing. His scam was that he was hired by Dubai developers to find out what developers in Qatar were working on. Then the Dubai developers would hire their entire teams—architects, construction project managers, engineers—right out from under the Qatar government, putting Qatar months and sometimes years behind."

"Are you talking hotels and shit?" Ryker asked.

The director nodded.

"Government?" Kostya asked. "I thought you said developers?"

"Almost every project developed in both Dubai and Qatar is totally or partially funded by their governments. There is a lot of competition to be a go-to travel destination in the Middle East."

"So, why did you call us in?" Kostya asked.

"I need you to track down Kraken and put a stop to them."

"Why?" Captain Hale asked. "Can't your man just contact them and say the mission is off?"

"The Kraken have gone dark. My former employee has tried contacting them every which way he knows how, and they haven't answered in the last thirty-eight hours. Trust me, he knows it's in his best interest to get ahold of either Ely or Ephram. Because if they succeed in their mission, my former agent is going to get the death penalty. Our people and the Brits in Dubai are sure they're protected, but they don't know the Kraken, your team does. I want you to stop them before they go through with their plan.

"In the meantime, we have our assets in Dubai. They will also look for Kraken." The director was looking directly at Kostya. "They will not approach them. They will provide any and all information they find to your team, Lieutenant Barona."

Captain Hale turned to look at the Omega Sky team. "Men, you have a half hour to board a plane to Dubai. You will not be able to go in armed."

"We have an asset in Dubai who will be able to provide you with weapons," the director assured Kostya.

The screen went blank for a moment, then once again Jase saw Kostya and his team on one square and Gideon on another.

"So, what's bothering you, Kostya?" Gideon asked. "Besides the fact that the CIA asset never came through with the weapons?"

"We know better than to depend on anybody but ourselves," Kostya said grimly. "What I'm wondering about is why would Ephram and the rest of his team go dark? Why wouldn't he keep in contact with his client when he knows the guy is CIA? He should be using him for information."

"One reason I can think of," Jase said. "One, he's worried that this guy is compromised."

"There's a second option," Tanner Robb spoke up. "They could have taken another job, and they don't care about missing out on the other seven and a half million."

"That's a lot of coin to walk away from," Jase said. "What's more, why not continue to talk to the CIA guy and lie to him?"

"Or do both jobs," Gideon said. "It sounds like they have enough members these days."

"That's what I'd do," Ryker said.

There was laughter. "Of course you would," Jase grinned. "You always like living life on the edge. How does Amy feel about that?" Amy was Ryker's fiancée.

"Are you kidding? Amy keeps him in line. Just wait til they have kids," Nolan smiled. "Then we'll see a whole new Ryker."

Jase thought about Lachlan and Amber. Yeah, if he had them in his life on a permanent basis, it would sure make him a hell of a lot more cautious in his personal life.

"Ryker. Gideon. Are either of you getting any closer to finding out about the C-4?" Kostya asked, interrupting the personal chatter.

"I'm working as a boss between the African and Sri Lankan labor camps. Mostly the African, because of my time in Africa." Ryker sounded frustrated. "I can't believe how bad this labor camp is, and I was in Sierra Leone during the Ebola outbreak."

"Yeah, but you don't show it. You fit right in with the

other bosses," Gideon assured him. Gideon turned to the others in the room. "You should see him. Ryker walks around like he's King Shit. He's using an Afrikaans accent. Nobody questions him. When he needs it, his pigeon Arabic is getting him by."

"I forgot Ryker spent time all over Africa," Jase admitted.

"Yeah, it's coming in handy," Gideon grinned over at Ryker. "There are some Sudanese and Rwanda here, and damned if he doesn't speak a couple of their languages. Meanwhile, I only have enough Arabic where I can understand just a few words."

"Yeah, you've always been a piker. So what's your situation like?" Kostya asked Gideon.

"Danmey Properties has done what all the other developers have done. They've created dorms. Imagine ant farms. Each dorm houses maybe a thousand workers. The dorms are separated by nationality or country. I'm relegated to the African one, obviously, bastards. Each dorm room houses fourteen of us. They've shoved seven bunkbeds in the room, with just enough space for a bucket in the corner when we can't make it the forty meters to the communal bathrooms."

"Gross," Landon said.

"You'd think those were bad, but I swear, the communal bathrooms are worse. Instead of sinks, there are three hoses that we're supposed to use to wash ourselves, fifteen urinals, and fifteen toilets, with eight of them overflowing with shit." Gideon looked up at everybody and then gave a reluctant chuckle. "So, no worse than any other mission."

"But those laborers. I can't believe they signed up for it, or that the UAE is allowing it," Tanner said in disgust. "Hell, the UAE is one of the richest countries in the world."

"This is how they do it. They get recruiters to go to their home country. The recruiters promise these guys great wages. Tell them they'll make enough that they'll be able to send money home to their families to lift them out of poverty. But as soon as the men arrive, their passports are oftentimes confiscated, then they're told that they have to work for one or two years to pay off the cost of their plane ride from Pakistan, India or wherever the fuck they're from," Gideon explained.

"Are you shitting me?" Mateo asked.

"Nope. So those first two years they make just enough money to subsist in the UAE, maybe a little extra so they can send some dirham home, but not the thousands like they were thinking. Certainly nothing like the recruiters promised. So, there they are, stuck in a foreign country, with their recruiters telling them that they are in debt to them not just for the plane ride, but also for their services of having brought them over to the UAE. Basically their first couple of years they're working for nothing. They're practically indentured servants, living in a hellhole, working ten to fourteen hours a day."

"The only saving grace is that it sounds better than some of the refugee camps we've seen," Jase sighed.

"Yeah, logically I know the refugee camp I saw in Yemen last year was worse, but this was done to these men and sometimes deliberately. They have tricked these fifteen- and sixteen-year-old boys, purposefully. They have no souls," Gideon bit out.

There was silence in the room. Finally Kostya broke it.

"Have you learned anything, Gideon?" Kostya asked.

"Yeah. The night before last there were three Americans floating around waving cash and asking to talk to anyone who worked on the Museum of the Future build. A few of the Pakistani laborers decided to take one of the Americans on and steal his money. Two of the laborers ended up dead, the other won't live long."

"What kind of information were they asking for?" Jonas wanted to know.

"Don't know that. Still trying to find out. There are too many of these dorms to work my way through. What's more, I'm relegated to the African area because of the color of my skin." He looked at Kostya. "We need more people."

"Who do you need?" their lieutenant asked.

"I need Jase and Mateo to get here so they can blend into some of the other areas. There are the Sri Lankan, Bangali, Indian, Pakistani, and even some Chinese groups. With your brown skin, you two could kind of pass as Pakastani or Bangladeshi. Both of those countries speak English. Ryker and I discussed it. We also need another man to act as one of the guards. We think Jonas would be good for this."

"How were you brought in?" Jase asked.

"Ryker brought me. Since he's a boss, it seemed normal for him to bring in a new recruit."

"How in the hell did they accept Ryker as a boss?" Jonas wanted to know.

Gideon gave a rough chuckle. "He just walks around with a stick up his ass, yells and shoves and behaves like an overall asshole. Everybody believes he's one of the guys in charge. When another boss comes to question him, he just says he's new. It's worked for him. He hasn't found out a damn thing, but at least he's brought me three candy bars."

There were some chuckles. "Have you been searching for the C-4?" Kostya asked.

"Nope. The camp is just too damned big," Ryker said. It was obvious he was frustrated. "Gideon and I are sorry that we're asking you to play day laborer."

Gideon nodded.

"As long as the candy bars are Snickers, I'm good, right, Mateo?"

"I've got you covered." Jonas smiled.

Mateo leaned over and bumped his fist with Jonas.

"Dammit, Ryker, all you gave me were those damned Almond Joys," Gideon bitched. "I want Snickers too."

Landon tipped his chair back and reached over to the overflowing basket of treats. He pulled out a bar. "Catch," he said to Gideon.

Everyone laughed when Gideon held up a Snickers bar and immediately opened it and bit off half of it.

"How are you looking for the C-4?" Tanner asked.

"The bosses have access to the supplies," Ryker

explained. "It'll look funny if we're searching through the different supply areas, but the laborers are always wandering around after shift."

"It's true," Gideon went on to explain. "You wouldn't think that after working twelve to fourteen hours that we would do anything other than hit our almost non-existent mattress. But, after working in the brutal sunlight, you really don't relish going and trying to sleep in a cramped box that feels like an oven. That's why so many of us walk around for a half hour before trying to sleep. One hundred and fifty kilos of C-4 should be housed somewhere, and when I find something promising, I tell Ryker."

"Yeah, then I bully or bullshit my way into the shed to take a look. But so far, nothing."

"Got it," Jonas nodded. "We can do that," he said as he pointed at Jase and Mateo.

"I'll bring the four of you in the company truck that I have waiting downstairs."

"How come upper management hasn't noticed they have one more supervisor working for them?" Tanner asked.

"There is only one manager for the whole camp. He's so overwhelmed that he doesn't know his ass from a hole in the ground, let alone who the different bosses are. The only time he pays attention is payday. Since we're not asking for money, we'll fly under the radar."

Jonas nodded.

"Sounds good," Kostya nodded. He turned to Jonas. "When are we going to get our weapons?"

Jonas jerked his thumb toward three golf bags in the corner of the room.

"I hope you all like to golf." He smirked.

Jase frowned, but Kostya smiled. He got up from the couch where he had been sitting and deposited his water bottle on the glass coffee table. When he went to the first set of clubs, he unzipped the hood, pulled out the one lonely driver, and flung it to the floor. Then with a sense of reverence he pulled out an M4 with a grenade launcher. Then another one, and another one. He carefully placed them against the wall, a grin on his face.

Sweet!

"Are you going to make me do all of the work?" Kostya asked as he looked over his shoulder at his team.

Soon twelve SIG Sauers, grenades, and MK 12 sniper rifles were proudly displayed.

"Jonas, you've outdone yourself," Kostya said. "I know this is looking a gift horse in the mouth, but do you have anything like comm systems or night vision?"

"Oh ye of little faith." Jonas's eyes sparkled. "Besides being avid golfers, all of us love video games. Therefore our gaming equipment will be arriving soon. This will include our headset and video game boxes. At least that's what it will look like. Then we'll be set."

"Before you ask, Boss," Jonas said as he leaned in to look Kostya in the eye. I grilled both the weapons supplier and the man who sold me the electronics. Neither of them admitted to selling anything similar to any Americans in the last month. I didn't believe them. But I needed their shit, so I wasn't going to push it.

"I don't suppose you could come up with clothes for Mateo and Jase to wear, could you?" Gideon asked.

"If you give me an hour, I could. I'm also going to see what I can do about getting some weapons that the three of you can conceal."

"That'd be much appreciated," Gideon sighed. "Most of the men are respectful of one another. After all, we're all in the same shitty situation. But there are a few that wouldn't hesitate trying to steal from the others and my cell phone is a hot ticket item."

8

Jonas took longer than expected, but when he *did* come back to the room, he had some ratty clothes and decent boots to go along with two suitcases that had prominent gaming logos on the front.

"I got these from another source," he said as he held up the suitcases. "Once again, I struck out. The guy who sold me the stuff wouldn't say whether he had sold anything similar to any other Americans in the last couple of weeks. I think the Kraken have either paid them to keep their mouths shut or terrified the hell out of them."

"I'm betting they scared the piss out of them," Ryker ground out. "I hate these motherfuckers."

"We're aware," Jase said.

Jonas handed Jase and Mateo a pair of boots. Both of them looked at them with distaste.

"Sorry guys, if you wear our normal boots, it'll be a dead giveaway. These are the nicest set of boots that you will be able to wear without drawing attention," Gideon told them.

"Which is why I got you a pair." Jonas handed a set to Gideon. "The reason I was gone so long was I had to go to three different stores to find boots big enough for Mateo. Jesus, what did they feed you down in Argentina?" Jonas asked.

"I didn't get my growth spurt until my family moved to Texas," Mateo said. "I blame it on the barbeque."

"Before you put the boots on, please take note of the interior sheath for your SOG Snarl knives. They fit perfectly. Because your boots aren't very high, your knives are relatively small, but they'll do in a pinch. Also, check out your belt. You're going to have to scuff it up, but you'll see that within the belt buckle is a concealed knife. So, guys, other than that, you're on your own."

"There's one more thing," Landon said seriously.

"What?" Kostya asked, leaning forward.

"They smell too good, Lieutenant. They're never going to believe they're new recruits when they smell that good."

"There's no 'Eau de Body Odor' in the bathroom, so what do you suggest we do?" Jase asked as he helped to divvy up the weapons into the new golf bags.

"I'll make you walk the last two miles to the dorm. In this heat, that should take care of things."

Jase shot Ryker the finger.

JASE WAS WANDERING AGAIN. After fifteen hours of digging a foundation, walking upright felt like a goddamned miracle. Hadn't anybody in this godforsaken country ever heard of an excavator? Or a pair of gloves?

Mateo was working on a different project. He was on the seventeenth floor, welding rebar, and he had to make a stink just to get a welding mask that had been fabricated by a seven-year-old fifty years ago. They'd only been on the job three days and Mateo had already seen one man injured so badly, he was sure he was going to die.

Up ahead, he finally saw who he'd been looking for. It was Vova. A kid with more brawn than sense. He couldn't be over twenty. He was there with his 'crew,' Faizan and Hazeem. What was scary was that Vova was the leader of their little gang.

He'd heard them talking in line to get to the toilet. Vova was being circumspect about the fact he was meeting up with someone who wanted information about the Museum of the Future. The kid didn't mention that the 'someone' was American, or that they were offering money, therefore none of the others in line paid him any attention. But Jase knew he'd hit pay dirt.

Jase had been walking back and forth in front of the south side of the dormitory where Vova and his friends were housed for the last hour and a half. Even though it was almost midnight, there were still many men wandering around, so it was easy enough for Jase to follow the three young men without being spotted.

They continued on until they got to the farthest building on the outskirts of the labor camp. Two fires were burning outside the dormitory, and Jase could smell meat being cooked. Vova slowed down and turned around, looking to see who else was in the area. Jase wandered close to one of the fires just as Vova and his friends drifted off around the corner of the building.

Jase waited a couple of minutes, then he walked over to the corner and stopped. He peered around the corner and couldn't see anything, but he could definitely hear an American talking.

"What part of the museum did you work on?"

"All of it," one of Vova's friends said. "I worked on the interior and the exterior."

"I worked only on the exterior," Vova's other friend said.

"I worked on the project until it was finished," Vova told the man. "I know plumbing, so I did more than my friends."

"You told me you did electrical!" the American shouted. "I need someone who worked with the lighting."

"Sir, nobody in the camps worked on the lighting," Vova stuttered. "That was all done by the UAE engineers."

"You lie. There had to be helpers. There aren't enough UAE engineers to do it all. Don't fucking lie to me. I want to know who worked on the lighting!"

"Sir, I promise you. We're not lying." Jase heard the fear in Vova's voice.

"You better find someone who worked on the lighting. I know which building you live in. I know which truck takes you to your work site. I will kill you if you don't get me the information I need. Do you understand me?"

"Yes, sir. But you must believe me."

"Yes, sir, believe all of us. We know nothing about—"

"Ahhh!"

It wasn't a gunshot, but Jase would bet his bottom dollar that one of the three men had just been pistol-whipped.

"That's just a taste of what will happen to you. I have friends who aren't nearly as patient as I am. You have twenty-four hours to bring me somebody who worked on the lighting in the Museum of the Future. Do you understand me? I'll meet you back here tomorrow."

"Yes, sir."

"Good!"

Jase heard loud footsteps that told him the man was leaving.

"Vova, what do we do? Faizan is bleeding badly."

Jase made a quick decision and moved to where Vova and his friends were. "Who was that man?" Jase asked as he knelt down next to the injured man. "Why did he have a gun?"

Jase pulled off the sash that Faizan used as a belt and wiped at the blood on his forehead so he could get a good look at his injury. He was going to have quite a goose-egg, but his skull wasn't cracked. The bleeding was coming from the scalp wound. They always bled like sons of bitches.

"I'm fine. Let me up," Faizon pushed at Jase.

Jase helped him to sit up.

"Tell me who that man was. He sounded American. Why were you meeting with him?" Jase was much older than the young men. He spoke with an authority that they easily responded to.

"I met him three nights ago. He said he knew I worked on the Museum of the Future, and he wanted me to find others who worked on the project as well. He said he would pay us a lot of money for information. He broke his promise."

"Of course he did. He was not to be trusted," Jase said with the best Indian accent he could muster. "What are your names?"

"I am Vova. They are Faizan and Hazeem. We all worked on the Museum of the Future, but he wants someone who worked on the lighting. None of the laborers worked on the lights."

"No, for that kind of work, it was done by UAE engineers," Hazeem said.

"What's going to happen if you don't find somebody that he wants?" Jase asked.

"He has a gun. He said that he would kill me."

"I think I know someone who worked on the lighting. When are you next meeting with the American? Will he give us money?"

"He promised money before. I don't know if he will give us money now that he showed us his gun."

"If he wants the information, he'll give us the money," Jase assured him.

After Jase's conversation with three young Pakistani men, he needed to get information to Kostya and the rest of the team... fast. He pulled out his cell phone and keyed into the Omega Sky group text.

> Jase: Pretty sure Kraken is on site. They've threatened to kill three teens if they don't find guys who worked at Future Museum. Kraken had gun.

> Kostya: Are they meeting again?

> Jase saw more dots coming up, so he waited to answer.

> Jonas: Where was this?

> Gideon: Did they mention anything about the C-4?

> Jase: They're meeting again in 24/hr, same place, furthest bldg. from camp, didn't mention C-4.

> Kostya: Do you have a plan? What do you need?

> Jase: I need Gideon to show up with me as guy who worked on lighting for museum. Meet 0130 at NE toilet. Meet with Kraken 0200. Will provide update after meeting.

> Kostya: Any other updates?

> Tanner: Met with CIA asset, they have no information on the Kraken.

> Kostya: No smartass comments. Anybody else with pertinent info?

> Braxton: Kraken is doing a background check on me. Might get hired on.

> Kostya: When will you know?

> Braxton: Tonight.

> Kostya: Keep me updated.

JASE WAITED FORTY SECONDS.

> Kostya: Denmay Team report back after meeting. If anyone else has something important that needs Denmay team, use group text, otherwise exclude them. Out.

WITH THAT DONE, Jase headed for his bunk. He could get in a good three hours of sleep before getting to dig in the dirt again.

WHY AM I NOT SURPRISED?

Jase was at the toilet at oh-one-twenty and there stood Ryker McQueen. He stood with his arms crossed over his chest, looking like he had a stick up his ass.

"Hurry the fuck up," he rumbled to one hapless worker. "This line is too long. Move it. Move it."

Then again, having everyone's attention focused on the asshole boss made things easier for Gideon and Jase to plan how they were going to play things with the Kraken.

If he was a Kraken.

At oh-one-thirty-two, Gideon came out of the toilet and barely avoided being shoved by Ryker. Instead, he hotfooted it over to the shadows where Jase was waiting.

"Why do you need me?" Gideon asked, getting to the crux of the matter.

"The American who was threatening the three Pakistanis was adamant that they needed to find someone who worked on the lighting for the Museum of the Future. The kids worked on the project, and they kept telling him that only UAE engineers worked on the lighting."

"They're probably right. I can't imagine any of the laborers they've brought in have the skill-set they need to run a complex lighting system that the museum needs."

"This American kept insisting that the UAE engineers would have needed helpers. That's where you come in. You can bullshit on this with the best of them. I figure once this guy establishes your legitimacy, he'll take you to some other guys, where you'll download your knowledge. I'll go with you."

"Like they'll go for that." Gideon rolled his eyes.

"Trust me, I'll insist."

"I'll go too," Ryker said as he walked up.

"No, you won't. There is no way that you'll be believed."

"Sure there is," Ryker said casually. "I'm the asshole boss who heard about a chance to make some money. You know damn good and well that they won't take any laborer seriously."

"Which makes it all the better," Gideon growled as he walked even further away from the group of men lined up for the toilet. "If they don't take us seriously, then we'll take them by surprise."

"Do you have a gun?"

I hate it when he's smug.

"You're going with us," Jase concurred.

9

Shit, shit, shit.

This is not going well.

By the time they'd got to the meeting place, the two of the Pakistani boy's bodies were lying in a pool of blood. The third boy, Vova, was kneeling in front of the bodies. An American stood over him. The man had the point of a knife digging into the boy's temple. The American was wearing combat gear, and it was easy to see the comm system he had around his neck.

"Welcome. Which one of you knows about the lights?"

Jase started talking in Arabic. "My friend here, he worked on the lighting on the Museum of the Future."

"English," the American shouted. "Don't try to bullshit me. You look like an Indian. You can speak English. If not you, the other one. Shove him forward. Make him speak English." He dug the knife into Vova's temple. Blood ran down his cheek, dripping onto his shoulder.

"I speak English. I helped with the lights," Gideon said. "What do you need to know?"

The American grinned. "Did you get that?" he asked the person on the other side of his mic.

Yep, they'd purchased communication equipment, just like our team had.

He nodded at whatever they said back to him.

Ryker stepped out of the shadows; he had a gun pointed at the American. "I'm with the two of them. Before you get any information, I want to be paid."

"Yeah, sure, like that's going to happen."

He pulled back the hair of Vova so he could look into the kid's wide, terrified eyes.

"Bye bye," he laughed. Then he shoved the dagger deep into Vova's temple. Jase watched in horror as the boy dropped to the ground. Goddammit, they'd sure played that wrong.

How could they have fucked that up so badly?!

"Now you've lost your leverage," Ryker said calmly. "Come with me," he said as he tapped Gideon and Jase's shoulders.

They heard a vehicle roll up behind the American. It was decision time. They needed to find out what the Kraken were up to.

"Ryker," Jase whispered.

"Agreed." Was all Ryker said.

Good. We're on the same wavelength. Jase wanted these motherfuckers dead.

"Mike, is everything going to plan?" a man with an English accent whispered loudly as he jumped out of the back of the truck.

"Stay right there," Ryker said. "Hands up, or I shoot your friend here."

The American killer sneered. "You won't do shit. You're after cash. You don't care if these two pieces of shit die. You're like me. You're in it for a payoff. Now, the only way either of us will get paid is if these two cough up information. Can you make them do that?"

"I own them. They know I hold the power of life or death over them. They'll talk." Ryker sounded stone cold.

"So, if I kill you, then I'll own them," the American smiled.

"Do you know how to talk to them? Have you been working with them for years? I don't think so. You need me. I'll get you what you need. But only if you pay me. I want a big enough payoff so I can live big in Thailand. I want two wives and a big house. You got it?"

"You get us the information we need, we'll pay you enough for four wives," the British man said as he came into view. He was holding a pistol aimed at Ryker. "Now come with us."

Jase, Gideon and Ryker had to step in the blood of the slain men to get to the truck.

"I'll take this," the American said as Ryker walked past him. Jase didn't have to look back to know he'd just taken Ryker's pistol.

All three of them were thrown into the back of a truck, and so began a long journey into the desert.

"Kind of stupid of them not to search us for any other weapons," Jase said as he pulled out his cell phone. Unfortunately, it was a burner phone with few features. But he could send a group text explaining what was happening.

"Jase, give the team these coordinates," Ryker said as he relayed them.

Of course, Ryker got the good phone.

"We need to make it seem like you have something to offer," Gideon said to Jase.

"Good luck with that," Ryker laughed.

Asshole

"They're a million different places that light fixtures were put in the museum. I'll figure out what they need, then I can say that I worked on it." Gideon frowned. "The problem's going to be that there is no way they'll believe I worked on any of the circuitry or programming." It was clear Gideon was thinking out loud.

"Me?" Jase asked.

"Maybe," Gideon looked Jase up and down. "Maybe because you know Arabic, we can say that you listened in more so that you could be of help. Let me think," Gideon said.

"Well, think fast," Ryker said. "The truck is slowing down."

"Jase, just follow my lead," Gideon snapped.

"Don't I always?"

"Isn't this kind of far out to be building the suburbs?" Ryker asked as they were shoved into a three-car garage.

"You talk too much for someone who wants money."

Jase got his first good look at the second man.

He was tall and thin, with a spider tattoo on his right cheek.

Yeah, he really blends in.

"So, I assume your name is Spider?" Ryker smirked. "Anybody stupid enough to get a tattoo on their face so they can be that easily identified can't be the leader of this goat fuck, so who in the hell should I be talking to?"

"Do you want to die? I can arrange that," Spider said in a jittery tone.

"Shut up, Spider. The man has a point." A woman with an Australian accent said as she stepped down from the door leading to the house. If that wasn't surprising enough, she was followed by Braxton.

"So, before bringing these three to our safe house, did you make sure they have the information that we require?" She was a blonde and gorgeous, in that thin, brittle way that always got on Jase's last nerve.

Spider looked over at the first dumbshit. They both looked scared.

The woman sighed and looked over her shoulder at Braxton. "You see why your resume interested me so much? I liked the fact that not only had you spent time in the field as a Delta Force, but you also did time in cyber security. Tell me, what would you have done before bringing these three to our safe house?"

"One of them would be missing at least a foot in order to verify the veracity of their information." Braxton said. "Normally I would start with a hand, but we're probably going to need that for the project."

"Ken. Spider. Do either of you know what the word 'veracity' means?" The blonde drawled.

Again, the two men looked at one another cluelessly.

"Maybe you should cut off one of *their* feet." She sounded bored. "Okay." She pointed at Ryker. "You sounded somewhat smart. Tell me what you have to offer."

"I know that veracity means truthfulness. As to what I'm offering. I'm giving you what you need. Omari here, was an electrical engineer in Rwanda. Darsh's father was an electrician in Bangladesh. They worked together on the lighting at the Museum of the Future."

"For how long?" the woman asked. She didn't sound bored now.

Neither Gideon nor Jase said anything. They looked at Ryker, as if waiting for his permission to speak.

The woman laughed. "You've trained them well."

"There have been many accidents on the job sites. They know that having a boss to look out for them will keep them safe."

"Braxton?" the woman nodded her head at their team member.

Braxton came over and hit Ryker in the face, and he landed on his ass. It was a light punch, but the way

Ryker bitched and moaned it made it seem like Braxton had broken his jaw.

What a drama queen.

Braxton grabbed Ryker by his shirt and punched him in the gut.

"All right," Ryker gasped. "I'll talk."

"Damn, I don't even get to use my knife," Braxton drawled.

"Spider, bring me a chair," the woman said. "This might take a while."

"Before I talk, I want a guarantee that I will get a half million USD transferred to my bank account," Ryker demanded.

The blonde laughed. "You know, just because you understand a big word, doesn't mean you're smart. A smart man would understand when he has a losing hand."

Jase grinned inwardly.

Here comes the bullshit.

"Kill me, and they'll never talk. They'd prefer to die than go back to the dorms without me. The other bosses know that they're with me. They won't die, but we have their passports. Trust me, their families will die."

The blonde sighed again.

"Let's see what they know. I'm not promising you anything until I know what I might be purchasing."

Ryker pushed out of Braxton's arms and turned to Jase. "Quit speaking Arabic, you fuck. Speak English. You too," he said, rounding on Gideon. "You answer every single question the lady has about the Museum of the Future. Your family's lives depend on it."

Gideon and Jase both nodded.

"Did you work on the interior or the exterior?" she asked with a smile.

"Both," Jase answered quickly. No way was he going to lose out on a fifty-fifty answer.

She nodded. "And you?" she asked, turning to Gideon.

"Yes, both."

She frowned. "It is my understanding that the lighting took a year to put into place. How could you have worked on both?"

"We worked on the circuitry for both. This did not require us working both inside and outside. We worked on testing the different switchgears at the beginning of the project, then as more power was needed, we assessed the load capacity."

"So, you know nothing about how the decorative lighting is displayed or turned on and off," she frowned. "This was handled by UAE employees?"

"Yes, the UAE engineers were the ones in charge of designing the multitude of displays that light up the eye of the museum. We touched none of this."

"Then you are useless to me," she spat out as she launched out of her chair.

"Ma'am, please tell us what you need," Jase said deferentially. "If we don't know what you need, how can we know how to serve you?" He tipped his head back and forth in the normal Indian fashion.

"I need the lights to go out when I need the lights to go out. There are too many to shoot out."

She looked at her men. "Get rid of them, and not in my garage." She started up the steps to her house.

"Ma'am, of course we can turn off the lights," Gideon said. "I told you we worked on the switchgears. Some of these will interrupt the flow of power to the museum. We can easily disable the switchgear that generates power to the eye's lighting, if that is what you are trying to do, but since construction is complete, sadly, we cannot get access."

The woman turned on her high heel and gave Gideon a narrow look. "Leave that to me."

10

THIS WAS NOT HOW IT WAS SUPPOSED TO BE GOING. JASE looked around the beautifully appointed bedroom and grimaced. Where in the hell were the others, and why was he in the middle of *Southern Living Magazine* here in Dubai? This certainly wasn't the house of the hard-hearted icicle.

He took three calming breaths, then did his best to roll toward the bed. It was pretty fucking hard to maintain your Zen when they hogtied your wrists to your ankles, and your fingers were inches away from touching your SOG Snarl knife. But Jase tried. He surely tried.

Aussie bitch didn't seem like someone who would have a rowing machine tucked behind her dust ruffle, but maybe the owner of the house would. He rolled the best he could until he nosed his way under the bed. He had to fight back bile.

Shit, I probably have a concussion from the hit on the back of the head that good ole Spider gave me.

Pushing that thought out of his mind, he shoved his head under the bed.

Jase fought back a sneeze. Then another one. Somebody wasn't doing a good job vacuuming under the bed. His eyes finally adjusted to the dark, and he saw three boxes. Department store boxes.

Great. Clothes.

"Aaaah...*Choo!*"

Fuck!

At least he'd muffled his sneeze into the thick Persian rug.

What in the hell? Something drifted out of the box nearest him. It was some kind of pink ribbon.

Lace?

Wait a minute, that is ribbon.

Jase shoved at the box some more, and more ribbon spilled out, this time white and silver. His heart beat a little faster. This couldn't be for real, could it?

How many times had his mom told him to get the wrapping paper box out from under her bed? Dozens? Wasn't there always tape and scissors in the box? A good *Southern Living* lady would certainly have tape and scissors in her wrapping paper box, wouldn't she?

Jase shoved his nose into the lid of the box, but that only pushed it farther away. He twisted himself around until the tips of his fingers could prod the lid off.

Success!

Come on. Be like my mom. Come on.

He worked at the box until it finally tilted. Ribbons, bows, tape, and wrapping paper fell onto his tied hands and ankles. Then he heard a thud and grinned. He wiggled his way down and felt around until his fingers felt the sharp edge of a blade.

Scissors!

Perfect.

After what seemed like forever, he was able to make enough of a slit in the plastic that he could yank his wrists apart. It took a minute too long as far as Jase was concerned to get enough feeling in his joints to move his hands so he could yank the tiny knife out of his boot and slice the restraints around his ankles.

He felt in his front pocket to see if his cell phone was still there, but it wasn't.

I guess Spider had to be good at something. Hitting me from behind and confiscating my cell phone are about it.

Now it was just a matter of getting the lay of the land so he could rescue Ryker and Gideon, figure out why they were so fucking interested in the Museum of the Future and find the damned C-4.

Jase got out from beneath the bed, wiped his bloody wrists on the bedspread, then went to the one door in the bedroom. After a minute of not hearing anything, he opened it just a little in order to take a look. Was that floral chintz wallpaper? Jesus, his mom would be in heaven.

He didn't see anybody in the hallway, nor did he hear anything. He pulled off his belt and took that bigger knife in his left hand, keeping the SOG Sarl knife in his boot. He silently went down the hall. Finally, he heard a voice. It was Braxton.

"I'm at your disposal. You tell me to wait. I wait. You

tell me to drive. I drive. You tell me to kill. I kill. I'm the world's best employee."

Shit, that was cold.

"I like you, Braxton."

Even when she tries to purr, it comes off like nails on a chalkboard, and I like an Aussie accent!

"There's a lot to like, if you get my meaning."

Ewwww.

"Work first."

"So, when am I going to meet Ely Roberts?" Braxton asked.

There was a long pause.

A long-ass pause.

"You're meeting me, isn't that enough?"

"Absolutely. Didn't mean to step on your lovely toes, darlin'."

God, he's laying it on thick.

"It's just that I've been trying to get on with this outfit for a while," Braxton explained. "Heard a lot of good things about Frank Sykes, and it was a hell of a disappointment to hear that he went head-to-head with a bunch of squids and ended up dead."

"That was before my time," the Aussie said. She didn't seem concerned. "Ely is more than enough man to keep things together. Under his leadership, the Elite has almost tripled in size."

"The Elite?" Braxton queried.

"The Kraken?" Jase could practically hear her shudder in distaste. "Such a Neanderthal name for an elite organization. Do you realize that most of our commissions are upwards of fifty million dollars? A business of that stature should have a name that is commiserate with its abilities."

"I'm pretty sure there is a pro wrestling team with that name."

"I'm pretty sure that if you want to become a part of this organization, you're going to need to show the proper respect."

"You're right. I'm sorry." Braxton sounded like a putz. Seemed like Ryker wasn't the only actor on the team.

"That's better. I like my men to show me the deference I'm due."

It all went quiet for over a minute. Jase took the chance to peek around the corner. Hot damn, there was a schefflera on the other side of the wall. He was hidden. But when he found a spot to look through the leaves, he shuddered. Braxton was holding the blonde in his arms. Or was it her holding him? Jase noticed she had his hair in a tight fist, and she was licking the underside of his jaw.

Once again, he was fighting not to throw up.

Braxton gracefully disentangled himself from her clutches. "You seemed to be complimenting Ely a lot. I don't want to be stepping in on another man's territory."

"I belong to myself." But she took two steps backward. "However, you're right. We need to be concentrating on the task at hand. I like how you handled that so-called 'boss'. The Rwandan seemed to be terrified of him, so you were right to keep the boss alive. How did you know all those technical things to ask the Rwandan?"

"I'm a man of many talents."

"Seriously."

"It was my time in cyber security. I had to learn a lot about a lot of things. That included switchgears. People might think they don't do much, but they control the electrical disconnect switches, fuses, or circuit—"

"Oh, do be quiet. You've already proved yourself."

"Just not the way I want to, Amanda."

"Again, down boy. Do you know enough that you could make this switchgear turn off the lights?"

"I couldn't identify a switchgear to save my life. What's more, I wouldn't know where they're housed." Braxton shrugged.

She sighed.

Jase heard the garage door motor. He watched Braxton stiffen. Was he going to continue to play along, or was he going to take her down?

"Sounds like dumb and dumber are back," he said. "Are you going to tell me why you need the lights to go out?"

"No. I don't like any of the team to know too much about anything. It's all about compartmentalization, you understand."

"I suppose that means you're not going to tell me about that crate of C-4 in the garage?"

"Dammit, I told those idiots to cover the markings on the crate. Can't they do anything right?"

Braxton chuckled. "Let me help you. No, they can't."

The door leading from the garage opened. Spider

stepped in first. His face was swollen. Then came a tall, handsome man in a suit. Jase noticed he was wearing the same kind of watch that Gideon had made him wear just a few days ago.

"Jesus, Amanda, where do you find these cretins?"

"What are you talking about? This idiot belongs to Ephram."

"Figures. Who do we have here?"

"This is Braxton Weller. Now this is one of my recruits. Former Delta Force with cyber security. He's been a big help finding out about lighting for the eye of the Museum of the Future."

"And our other project?"

She paused. Jase would bet his last dollar she was going to lie. "He doesn't know anything about that project. I'm using the normal protocols."

He moved in front of her, then lifted her chin.

"You're such a good girl."

She looked up at him through her lashes.

"Thank you, Daddy."

Jase swallowed fast.

I am definitely going to be sick.

11

"SHOW ME WHAT YOU'VE GOT,"

The bitch giggled. Jase looked over at Braxton. He was stone-faced. Spider looked pissed. That was good. Where was the other cretin?

The blonde turned to Spider. "Spider—" she started. "Oh, never mind."

She turned her gaze to Braxton. "Braxton, you get our guests. Set them up around the dining room table. Spider, get rid of the flowers and the tablecloth." She turned to Ely. "Seriously, can't we get a different safe house?"

"Nobody will ever suspect that we're using the British Ambassador's mother-in-law's house. She's stays in Georgia most of the time, anyway. So, this is perfect."

"It gives me hives."

He cupped her face and leaned in. His kiss was gentle. "Just a few more days and we get to leave Dubai," he whispered. "And, because of you, we're going to leave seven and a half million dollars richer. That's on top of the fifty million."

"And don't you forget it," she sighed up at him. "Never, ever, leave money on the table."

"That's my girl."

Braxton cleared his throat.

Ely looked over his shoulder at Braxton. "I believe my girl gave you an order."

"You're right, she did." He put two fingers to his forehead, pulled a gun out of his shoulder holster, and headed for the hallway. He gave a piercing glance at Jase as he rounded the corner. Jase followed him as they went to the room he had been tied up in and closed the door behind them.

"Damn good thing I still have some zip ties with me," Braxton said as Jase turned around and gave his wrists to Braxton to bind.

"How much did you hear?"

"Started with you saying, 'tell me to kill, I kill'. Pretty cold stuff, Brax."

"Okay, so you know about the C-4. That's good."

"And that you can kiss a psychotic icicle. How was that?"

"I don't even want to think about it," Braxton shivered. "Thank God her 'Daddy's' here. Which is another thing I don't want to think about. Look, I really had to rough up Ryker, otherwise Spider and that other idiot were going to do it. Gideon is fine. He played up meek and scared perfectly."

"Do you know what's next?"

"No. But wanting the lights to go out seems to me

like a they need a fast exit. Maybe some kind of kidnapping?" Braxton guessed.

"Or it could be an assassination," Jase countered. "We've got to get the info to Kostya so he can see what or who is going on in the next few days at the museum."

"The fact that the C-4 is here and they're talking about the next payment of seven and a half million says that they still intend to go through with the bombing of the embassies."

Jase winced when the zip-ties bit into his bloody wrists. "Agreed."

"Okay, let's go get Ryker and Gideon," Braxton said as he turned Jase to the door.

They went to the end of the hall to what had to be the master bedroom.

"Hurry it up. We don't have all day," Braxton said loudly enough so his voice could be carried to Ely and Amanda.

"I'm sorry, sir," Jase said apologetically, making sure his voice could be heard as well.

Braxton slammed open the door. "Look at the mess you've made," he yelled. "You've puked all over the floor."

Jase felt a strong sense of déjà vu as he took in the throw up on the carpet. But instead of a little boy and girl looking up at him, there was Ryker, staring at him with one good eye. The other was swollen shut. There was blood matted in his hair, and vomit was caked to his chin.

Huddled in a corner was Gideon. His hands behind his back. Jase was surrounded by actors.

"I'm going to need to get him cleaned up before I take him back to the table."

Braxton slammed the door shut.

As soon as the door was closed, everybody started moving. Gideon stood up.

"How'd you get out of your ties?" Jase asked.

"Brax conveniently hogtied me so my hands could reach the knife in my boot." Gideon said as he shook his hands to get the circulation flowing.

Braxton was helping Ryker get up off the floor. "Nice job with the puke," Braxton complimented their teammate.

"Yeah, well, it didn't take that much effort. Can't wait to do some hand-to-hand training with you when we get back to Little Creek." Ryker walked toward the connecting bathroom. Jase followed him.

After Ryker was finished wiping off the blood and vomit from his face, and rinsing his mouth, he used a washcloth to wipe off the blood from Jase's face too.

"We make a fine pair, don't we?" Ryker gave him a half-hearted grin in the mirror.

"Ryker, get out here. I need to get this zip-tie on you, so I can take you out for questioning."

"How fun," came Ryker's sarcastic answer. He looked over at Gideon as he followed Jase out of the bathroom.

"Anybody got an idea on how to play this?" Braxton asked.

"I've got an idea. Just follow my lead," Ryker said.

"Now I know how my brothers always felt," Jase mumbled.

"Gideon, you lead the way. Jase, you help me. Brax'll follow the three of us with his gun."

"Got it," Jase said.

Gideon opened the door and started down the hall. Jase followed and Ryker leaned on him, making it seem like he was severely injured. Braxton followed the trio, holding his gun. There were two more men besides Ely, Spider, and the Snow Queen. They were so big; it looked like they could make up the entire defensive line for the Cavaliers. One was wearing a barely there black tank top, and the other had on a black headband. Jase knew they were trying for the Rambo look from the eighties, but since they were both sporting short hair, he couldn't help thinking of the Olivia Newton John Let's Get Physical music video.

Please don't let me laugh.

"Spider. Braxton. Make our guests comfortable," Ely said.

Before Spider had a chance to do anything, Braxton had the three of them slammed into the dining room chairs, facing Amanda and Ely.

"He's the one with the knowledge. He's an engineer." Amanda said, pointing a red tipped nail at Gideon.

"So, why are the other two breathing?" Ely asked.

She pointed at Jase. "He's the helper. Apparently, it's a big job, and the engineer needs help."

"And the one who's beat to shit?" Ely asked.

"He's the muscle who keeps them in line. He's also a pain in my ass because he wants money."

"Fucking right I do," Ryker bellowed in his Afrikaans accent. He spit blood onto the shiny dining room table. "These two won't take a shit unless I tell them to."

Ely laughed. "We're the ones with the guns. We kill you and they'll do what I say."

"Doesn't work like that, old man. Me and my bras back at the camp hold on to their passports. We know where their families are. My brothers won't hesitate to have their families killed if something happens to me. These two know it. You're stuck with me," Ryker gave a lopsided grin from his swollen mouth.

Ely looked upward as if he were looking for divine intervention.

"Fine. I need the three of you."

"And I need my money. A half million USD, transferred to my bank. I want it before they start the job on the Museum of the Future."

"Teach him to show me some manners." Ely commanded Spider. "But don't kill him."

Spider went for his gun.

Braxton pulled out his knife and punched it into Ryker's upper thigh before Spider had a chance to pull out his gun from his holster.

Ryker screamed. And screamed. And screamed.

What was he going for, an Oscar?

Now came the tears.

Jase looked at Braxton's knife. Only a half inch of the tip was bloody. He wiped it off on the sleeve of Ryker's shirt before anybody else could notice.

"You're going to regret this!" Ryker shouted in between sobs.

"Does he even have balls?" Amanda asked Ely.

"I don't know. Do you want to check, darling?"

"You fucks still owe me money," Ryker gasped. "Now the price just went up."

Amanda and Ely laughed. "Maybe he has one ball," Ely said.

"Want me to cut off a finger?" Braxton asked.

"We don't have time. I want to find out where the switchgears are so we can come up with a plan on how to get to them," Ely explained. "You two," he nodded to Gideon and Jase. "You're going to help figure out how to get by the security and get to wherever the switchgears are. Meanwhile, we'll keep your boss here as an incentive for you to do what we require. Got it?"

Jase and Gideon both nodded.

"Bull? Rob? You will go with them. Get them suited up so they blend in. I want you to make sure that the four of you can bypass security and make it to the switchgears. And for God's sake, while you're suiting them up, find yourselves something to wear, something that will blend in!"

"Got it, boss."

"What about me?" Braxton asked.

"We have another project that you should be able to help us with." Ely smiled.

12

THE MUSEUM OF THE FUTURE WAS HUGE. THERE WAS NO need to ask Kostya what was going on. It was perfectly clear. Signs were up everywhere. The youngest and most popular Prince of the Dubai royal family was going to be giving a speech about a new exhibit opening up. The speech would be the next evening. He was bringing his wife and three children.

Were the Kraken out of their mind? Scratch that. It was fifty million dollars. They were just greedy. But did they really think they'd make it out of the country alive?

"I don't know how to get to the switchgears. Normally they would be outside of the building for cooler airflow, but not in this desert heat," Gideon whispered to Jase as they followed tourists through the Oman Across the Ages display. "It has to be in the basement."

"What are you talking about?" Bull demanded to know. He pushed his way between them.

"You need to back off, people are looking," Jase frowned. "We can't draw attention to ourselves. Also, you need to whisper."

"Then you need to walk with us."

"No," Gideon disagreed. "We look like wealthy business executives, and you look like our security. We wouldn't walk together. You would walk behind us." Gideon gestured to his and Jase's bespoke suits.

"Don't blow this," Jase hissed. "Amanda and Ely will have your balls."

Bull drifted back to stand next to Rob.

"I need a tablet or a smartphone," Gideon said to Jase. "I should be able to call up the schematics to this place, or at least get in touch with one of the other SEAL team's tech ops and they can grab them."

Jase looked up and saw the sign to the Museum of the Future's Heal Institute DNA library. As he remembered, it was dark with glowing strands of DNA. A perfect spot to do some pick-pocketing. He just wished that Jonas was around. This was so much more his area of expertise.

Jase lifted his chin, and Gideon followed him into an elevator to the correct level. They were soon ensconced in another world. If he wasn't on a mission to find somebody's backpack or purse, he'd find the whole place fascinating.

"I can't believe he did that. You need to kick him to the curb!" Everybody was staring at the young girl on the phone.

"Fuck him. He doesn't deserve your time. Your vajajay is worth diamonds, not cubic zirconia. He doesn't get entry with something that doesn't cut glass. Are you hearing me, Tiffany?"

She paused for just a moment to take a breath, and Jase saw his target. A young man with a Crimson Tide logo on his backpack was standing there with his mouth and backpack open, listening to the girl in disbelief. Jase needed a tablet that was in English, hopefully without facial recognition, to get into it.

"I don't care if he has muscles to die for. He probably takes steroids and has a needle dick. I'm talking pinkie size. He's going to have to give you a big-assed diamond to make up for it."

Just as Jace was plucking the tablet out of the young man's backpack, a security guard came up to the rude girl and the conversation about genitalia ended. Gideon's eyes were glowing with amusement when he got back to him.

"Let's move," Jase said. "Do you need light?"

"Nope. Need to do this where nobody will interrupt me."

"Vault of Life, here we come." Jase guided them to another elevator. Rob and Bull barely made it on with them.

"Where did you get that?" Rob asked.

"It was a birthday present," Jase said. "Omari has always wanted a tablet."

"Do not listen to him," Gideon said in a subservient tone. "I must have this to determine the new schematics of the building. Much has changed since I was here. We must move fast, yes?"

Rob looked suspicious, but Bull nodded. "Good thinking."

Jase bit back another sarcastic comment. He needed to remember he was subservient as well.

They stepped out of the elevator and were once again in another world. The vast room was dark, except for the thousands of elevated neon specimen jars showing all the different species of life.

Gideon ignored the spectacle and looked for a wall that he could sit against and peruse the internet or get ahold of his counterparts on one or all of the SEAL teams in the United States. Jase noticed that even Bull and Robb were looking up at the jars. They were as entranced as the other visitors.

Jase wandered far away from Gideon, wanting the two goons to follow him, so that Gideon could do his thing. He knew damn good and well that he wouldn't just be conferring about the schematics of the place, he'd be informing Kostya of everything that was going down. He knew his lieutenant; he'd find a way to get hold of Braxton without blowing his cover and figure out what was going on with the C-4.

As for the assassination or kidnapping, Gideon and Jase had a good chance of taking this down, but more help was always appreciated. What's more, they needed to find out who was behind this fifty million dollar hit.

"Did you get to the switchgears?" Ely asked.

Ryker looked like he was going to puke again, and

Spider looked happy. Apparently, he had been working over their teammate some more.

"They got there, boss," Rob answered.

"There is going to be more security tomorrow night. We're going to bring in more team members to support this effort, as well as Roger."

Jase wondered where Amanda was. He hadn't seen the crate with the C-4 when he'd been brought back through the garage.

"Who here cooks?" Ely asked.

The two bodybuilders looked at Spider.

"Make us dinner," Ely demanded. "Enough for our prisoners, too." He glanced over at Jase and Gideon. "Get out of your clothes. You're going to need them for tomorrow night." Then he pointed to the tablet in Gideon's hand. "What's that?"

"I needed it to look up the schematics of the building, sir. There had been much construction since I was last there."

"Where did you get it?" Ely barked.

Jase bobbed his head. "I stole it, sir. We desperately needed it."

Ely stormed over to him and backhanded him. "That was very risky." Then he turned his attention back to Gideon. "You got what you needed?"

"Yes, Sir."

"Good. Give me the tablet. You can have it back tomorrow night."

Gideon handed it over. Jase was confident he had hidden all of his correspondence with the other SEAL teams and whatever else he'd been busy doing.

"You heard me. Get out of those clothes." Ely waved them to a back room. "Take him with you," he waved to Ryker.

Ryker lifted his head from the dining room table. "Tomorrow night," he slurred as he looked at Gideon and Jase. "Isn't that handy? That's when the word will go out to kill your families."

"Please no, Sir," Gideon begged. "We must do this, otherwise we will be killed."

"Your choice," Ryker said. "Your life, or the lives of your women and children."

Jase turned to Ely. "I'm sorry, sir. I cannot continue."

Ely backhanded him again. And again.

Jase didn't flinch.

"Now, do you want my banking information?" Ryker asked.

Ely turned to Rob. "Can't you do what this helper does?"

"I don't know, Boss. Everything in the basement looked pretty complicated to me."

Ely rounded on Gideon. "And you?"

"I have three sons and one daughter. They are my world."

"Fuck!" He stormed into the kitchen, and Jase heard him rustling through a drawer. He came back out with a piece of stationery and a pink pen. "Write down your banking information."

Ryker did. It was an actual account that the CIA always had available to them. You never knew what you might need on a mission.

ONCE AGAIN, they were hog-tied in the master bedroom, this time without their boots.

"What were you able to tell Kostya?" Jase asked Gideon in a hushed voice.

"Everything."

"Define everything," Ryker growled. "Does that include how Brax beat the shit out of me and stabbed me?"

"Such a baby," Jase shook his head and gave him a fake, sympathetic look.

"Would you two shut it?" Gideon snarled. "Here's what I know. Brax reported to him. The C-4 was put on an orange tanker truck heading back into the city. Should have been easy enough to stop, unfortunately there is a convoy of at least one hundred orange tankers headed back to the city every day. Mostly to the Burj Khalifa."

"Why in the hell are oil tankers going to the Burj Khalifa? The tower runs on electricity," Jase pointed out.

"Yep, the tallest building in the world is perfectly modern, except it is not connected to a sewer system. Those trucks pick up all the sewage each day. Tons of it. Then they truck it out to a sewage treatment plant out in the desert, then turn back around and do it all over again."

"Are you shitting me?" Ryker asked.

Jase and Gideon both chuckled softly.

"Okay, poor choice of words. But still, you're messing with me, right?"

"I am not. So, the C-4 is on one of those trucks, coming into the city. Brax doesn't know which one. We're still going on the assumption that the Kraken is going to use this to blow up the US Consulate and the British Embassy. We just don't have a timeline."

"If we stop the C-4, then we stop the plan," Jase said.

"That's how Kostya sees it, too. Apparently, the trucks never deviate from their routes, so the C-4 is going to be handed off in the basement of the Burj. That means that someone from our team is going to need to be there to intercept it."

"And here I thought I had the shittiest part of this assignment," Ryker laughed. "Do we know who Kostya is sending in?"

"Keegan, Tanner, and Landon are going in. There need to be three men because that area is huge."

"How many tons of waste a day is there?" Jase asked.

"How should Gideon know?" Ryker looked at Jase like he was crazy.

"Seven tons of excrement, then with water for brushing your teeth, showers and so on, it comes to about fifteen tons."

"Of course, he knows, he's Gideon," Jase smirked.

Ryker shuddered. "Please tell me you don't share this kind of information with Jada, cause if you do, you're never getting laid again."

"It is not my vast amounts of knowledge that my

woman is after me for," Gideon grumbled. "Dammit, I want to get home."

"Me too," Ryker agreed.

"Me three." Jase said emphatically.

"How come I'm thinking you've been holding out on us?" Ryker looked over at Jase in surprise.

"I've been dating a single mother who is skittish about relationships, and extremely skittish about Navy SEALs. I think she heard about every oat you ever sowed, Ryker."

"I wasn't that bad," he protested.

"Yes, you were," Gideon disagreed. "Now enough girl talk. Brax is still with Amanda."

"I saw them kiss. I hope she's not demanding anything more of him," Jase winced.

"I bet he'd prefer to be working in the shit basement," Ryker said.

"This still sounds like girl talk," Gideon admonished them both. "Kostya's bringing everybody else to the museum tomorrow. The good news is, we'll have an idea when they'll strike. Hopefully, we can get more information while we're here, whiling away the hours."

"Yeah, like who ordered the hit." Jase rubbed his shoulder against the carpet, trying to scratch an itch.

"Also, finding out how they plan to take out the prinsh, I mean prince, would be nice," Ryker commented. He rolled over three times until his front was nestled against Jase's back. "I think it's about time we did a little reconnaissance. Unbuckle my belt."

"Hot damn. You still have your knife!"

As soon as the words were out of Jase's mouth, he realized they meant jack shit. Even if they cut themselves out of their restraints to go look around, there was no way the three of them could tie themselves back up.

Shit.

He looked at Gideon and Ryker and saw they had realized the same thing.

"It's worth the risk," Gideon said.

"Agreed," Ryker nodded. "We need intelligence. We can't just follow these idiots around blind and wait for something to happen."

While they were talking, Jase was unbuckling Ryker's belt and unhooking the knife.

"Ouch, be careful with that shing. I mean thing," Ryker said.

Jase laughed. He knew damn good and well that Ryker was only saying that in order to make him and Gideon laugh.

After Jase got Ryker's hands untied, Ryker cut the rest of them loose. He looked down at his watch. "It's a minute past twenty-two-hundred hours. Do we wait?"

Jase nodded. "I say we wait until zero hundred."

Ryker and Gideon nodded.

"Time for shut eye. Give me your watch, Ryker. I'll wake you both at go-time," Jase ordered.

"No, you two sleep. I rested while you were at the museum," Ryker protested.

Gideon snorted. "Passing out from blood loss isn't sleeping. Give Jase your watch, shut-up and sleep."

13

"Nobody ever locks their tablets. What's up with that?" Gideon mumbled.

Ryker was at the mouth of the hallway to the bedrooms, keeping watch for activity. Everything was quiet, but they needed to make sure nobody caught them by surprise. When Jase checked the three-car garage, there was only a sedan. It seemed like it would only be Ely who was with them, but they still needed to be careful.

Jase was now planted at the curtains in the study, watching to see if anyone was driving up to the house. They were at the end of a cul-de-sac in a well-to-do neighborhood.

Totally bizarre.

"Don't look a gift horse in the mouth. Be happy you can access Ely's information. Find out what's going on. Does he have a file named plot to kill the prince? Can you e-mail it to Kostya so we can get out of here?"

"Come here," Gideon motioned.

Jase went to look over Gideon's shoulders. He didn't need to be watching outside. Anybody who would be coming to the house would use the garage doors. The sound of the garage door opening would be enough of a clue to get their happy asses back to the bedroom.

"Whatchya got?"

"I think I have their personnel roster. Ely and Amanda aren't on it. I don't see someone named Spider or Bull, but I do see a Robert Gibbons, with a date beside his name. It was five months ago. There are forty-seven names."

"E-mail it to yourself."

"Kane's downloading the entire hard-drive to himself as we speak, so that's covered. But what scaring me is that there are forty-seven names on it. Why would they need to recruit Brax?"

"Maybe they have enough jobs world-wide that they needed another man here in Dubai," Jase said hopefully.

"Maybe."

"Anything else?"

"Ely hasn't encrypted anything, so he's making it easy. Wait a minute. Are you shitting me?"

"What?"

"He's got everything filed in his Outlook. He's got a file titled UAE, and sub-directories of Future, Consul, Revenue, Expenses. It can't be this fucking easy. It just can't be."

Jase continued to look over his friend's shoulder. He watched him open the revenue folder and then saw an encrypted e-mail. Gideon double-clicked on it. It required a password.

Gideon looked at Jase. "This is it. The dumbass is putting his payment e-mails in an Outlook file called revenue. I could kiss the guy, but Amanda already has that covered."

Jase looked around at the study. "I bet if you moved one pencil an inch to the left, his head would explode."

"Yeah, he definitely has OCD tendencies."

"Did you find anything else relating to this evening's assassination or kidnapping or what's going on with the American consulate's office?"

"I need time to really go through this tablet. Maybe an hour or two and I'd find something. Or less because he'll have it so conveniently labeled."

"I get what you're saying, but what about Ryker? As funny as he's being, I want to get him to a hospital. He puked again while we were in here."

"How in the hell do you know that?"

"I heard him hurl into the plant by the hallway. Also, Mr. Comedian slurred his words a bit. He tried to play it off, but he did it."

"I'll check his pupils when we get back to the room. In the meantime, I need to get my suspicions about Brax to Kostya. I don't know Brax's number, and even if I did, I'd worry he was being monitored. Let me send off an e-mail."

Jase nodded. God, he was sick of this fussy Southern house in the desert.

"You look like you want to get out of here as much as I do," Gideon commented.

Jase looked down at the time on the screen. Three hundred. "Probably even more, but until we have something substantial, we need to stick with this," Jase told his team's second in command.

Gideon looked up from the tablet. "I agree. The one caveat is, if we need to get Ryker to a hospital, then we come up with another plan."

"Agreed," Jase nodded. "What are we going to do about tying ourselves back up?" Jase whispered as they headed for the hallway.

They looked up and saw Ryker holding up a handful of zip-ties with a lopsided grin. Too lopsided, in Jase's opinion.

"Where'd you get those?"

"I went through the three duffel bags in the living room. I'm figuring they were the muscle twins and Spider's. I hit pay dirt. No guns, but" he held up a set of brass knuckles. Then he held up three steak knives that he had obviously taken from the kitchen. "I love a woman who keeps her implements sharpened."

"Nice job," Jase said as he took a knife from Ryker.

"Thanks," Ryker whispered as they closed the door to their room. He frowned as Gideon dragged him into the master bathroom and turned on the light.

"Fuck man, your right pupil is bigger than your left," Gideon exclaimed in a low voice.

Ryker planted his hands on the bathroom counter and looked in the mirror.

"It's minimal. This is what we call a Junior Varsity concussion where I come from. If you were playing JV, this would have you benched. If you were varsity, they'd slap your ass and send you back out onto the field."

"That's not funny," Jase growled.

"Sure, it is," Ryker grinned. "Your new girlfriend just isn't giving you any yet, so you don't have a sense of humor."

Jase went hot as Ryker talked about Bonnie. "Shut the fuck up, McQueen," Jase hissed. "The high school concussion schtick isn't funny, the joke about my woman isn't funny, and I'd normally hit you except you have a fucking concussion!"

"Keep your voice down," Gideon shushed him.

Ryker opened his mouth to respond. "You just shut up," Gideon pointed at Ryker. "He's right."

"Goddamned right, I'm right. I heard you yacking up your guts into the plant. Like Ely isn't going to notice that stench. Good thinking, genius. That is not the move of a SEAL, that's the move of a JV football player."

Ryker deflated right in front of Jase.

"Look, it's not that bad. We have a job to do, and I can hold up my end. All I have to do is yell at you two and look pretty."

"You also have to continue to prove to Ely that you're worthwhile, so he doesn't decide to kill you."

Ryker shrugged. "There is that."

Gideon slammed off the lights. "You two hit the floor. I'm tying you up, then I'm going to go clean the puke out of the plant. I'll keep first watch. I want to check that the download finishes on the tablet."

Jase wanted to disagree, but what Gideon said made

sense. He turned around and crossed his wrists behind his back...again.

JASE WAS awake when their door was flung open and the steroid freaks came in, looking pissed. They were followed by Ely.

Jase stopped his first inclination to be a smart-ass. He needed to remember that he was a laborer from India. He looked over his shoulder at Ryker and waited for him to be the smartass. No such luck. He was having trouble lifting his head.

"Our boss is sick," Jase said in a troubled tone. "He cannot be sick, otherwise he cannot make calls to the other bosses in the camp." Jase looked over at Gideon for back-up.

"Why aren't you tied up, right?" Ely demanded to know. He pointed at Gideon and tipped his chin to one of the behemoths.

"What?" Gideon asked.

Rob went over to Gideon and grabbed at the ties on his wrists and ankles. They were both connected to one another, but in the front of his body, not the back of his body.

"They look good to me."

"He's not tied like the other two. His hands are in the front, you imbecile. Who tied them?"

"Spider. Then we all went back to the city to see if we could find the lost package."

Ely stepped up to Rob. "Who asked you to do that?"

he asked softly. "We have more than enough staff working on that project."

Rob looked scared. For that matter, so did Bull.

"Sorry Mr. Roberts. We were just following orders," Rob said in a squeaky voice.

"But not *my* orders. My orders were that you were to stay outside on guard. Weren't they? Where is Spider?" he asked softly.

"He left. He was mad because you'd hit him and—"

Ely's fist snapped out and back. It was an expertly deployed Krav Maga hit to the crotch. Rob toppled over like a tree. He let out a high-pitched squeal that would have dogs barking for miles.

Ely stuck his toe into Gideon's gut and pushed him onto his back as he pulled out his phone.

"Amanda?"

There was a pause as he listened to the Popsicle.

"Take a breath."

He waited again.

"What do you mean you can't find the C-4? Your job was to kill the plant and put the C-4 on a truck heading for the city."

Ely paused and Jase saw he was getting pissed. He used the toe of his dress shoe to prod at Gideon from time to time.

"I don't care what Ephram tells you to do, you listen to me. It was his idiot plan to have you put the C-4 on one of those trucks, wasn't it? Make him and his team find it."

Everybody in the room could hear her high-pitched yammering. They couldn't make out exactly what she was saying, but her tone was unmistakable. She was angry.

"I take your point. You're right, he wouldn't go through with the job, and we would be out the money. Don't kill Braxton yet. Use him. Kill him after you've reacquired the explosives and positioned them where we want them."

That must have pacified her, because now she was talking softly.

"I'm keeping Bull with me." Ely pulled out a deadly looking dagger from a sheath underneath his pant leg. Gideon froze. He was ready to attack if Ely made any move against the three SEALs.

Ely stepped over Gideon to where Rob was still rolling around in agony. "I'm going to pull in a few more men," Ely told Amanda.

He paused as he looked at Rob and listened to the human icicle.

"Yes, more than our hit team. I want more good people around me when the lights go down."

He kept his phone up to his ear, looking bored at whatever else Amanda had to say. In a swift move, he jammed his shoe on the side of Rob's neck, forcing his head against the floor.

"Yes. If you think you need to pull in a couple of more, by all means, coordinate that," he smiled. He positioned the point of his dagger into the tender flesh of Rob's temple. Rob jerked, trying to get away, and Ely smiled, then shoved the dagger through the man's brain.

"Amanda, I have a couple of things I need to clean-up here. Call me when you reacquire the C-4."

He paused. "What?"

He smiled and chuckled softly. "Me? No, I wouldn't handle things the way Sergei is."

Jase saw his face get soft. "I know you love me, Amanda."

She said something else.

"I'm just saying that besides making the man suffer, I would make sure my woman got what she deserved as well."

Oooops, bitch, better not give the game away.

"Enough of this Amanda. I have things to do, and so do you."

Ely straightened up, pocketing his cell phone and leaving the dagger lodged in Rob's brain. "Bull, I need you to call Lawrence and Gil. They need to bring the new recruit they've been training. I want them here immediately. They'll come with us tonight."

Bull looked lost.

"Earnhart! Pull yourself together, otherwise I'll kill you as well. I need you to call Lawrence and Gil. Tell them to bring their new recruit. I want them here in twenty minutes."

"But they're in Dubai, Sir. That's a ninety-minute drive."

"So, you do want me to kill you? Or do you want to do what I ask you to do?" Ely questioned his not so smart employee.

"I'll get them here," Bull said as he scurried out of the bedroom.

"And here I thought I was going to kill you," Ely

said as he looked at Ryker. "Instead, I'm thinking you might fill in for Spider tonight. It wasn't the lead role, but it was going to be a memorable one. Think Macbeth."

14

Jase looked down at his expensive watch. It was fifteen hundred thirty-three. He and Gideon were in an air-conditioned limousine with Ely. They were back in their expensive suits.

"You saw your man make his phone calls to his counterpart. Your families are safe for another day. If you don't do exactly what I say, there will be no call tomorrow. Do you understand me?"

Jase did a head bob, and Gideon nodded.

"I haven't killed him. Hopefully, he'll last long enough so that I can have you all dumped back at the labor camps."

Jase grimaced. Ryker needed a hospital. His right pupil was blown, and it was taking all he had to stay upright. When Bull had pressed him into the front seat of the most immaculate landscape truck Jase had ever seen, it looked like Ryker might puke again. How was that even possible since he had eaten none of the food they'd been given? He'd watched as they drove away, with grass clippings floating away behind them.

Jase tried not to worry about Ryker, and instead think about how they planned to assassinate the prince at that evening's ceremony. After hearing the conversation between Amanda and Ely, Jase knew this wasn't a kidnapping attempt. As they came up to the museum, their limousine was whisked to the front area where dignitaries were dropped off.

When they were ushered into the building Ely was flagged down by three other men in business suits.

Nothing clandestine going on here.

"You will go with them," Ely says as he directs Jase and Gideon to a short black man and two tall Caucasians, one blonde, one red-head. "Follow them closely," he says to the shorter of the three. He is obviously the man in charge. "Fifteen minutes after I call, the power to the lights need to be shut off. Do you understand me? Without that happening, Roger and Luc cannot depart."

The black man gave Ely a serious look. "I understand. And our orders after that remain the same?"

"Yes."

Apparently, everyone thought two laborers were dumb. Jase managed not to roll his eyes.

Jase glanced over at Gideon, then looked over at the robot fish flying toward them above the lobby floor. Yep, they planned to kill them as soon as they'd accomplished their mission.

Jase spotted Nolan when they were in front of a display of the Amazon forest. When he looked over at Gideon, his teammate just nodded as he kept his focus on the display in front of them.

Jase tapped the red-head on the arm.

"Toilet."

"No."

"Toilet," he said again.

The red-head got in his face and growled. "No."

"I either crap my pants, or one of you goes with me to the toilet," Jase gritted out the words.

"I'll take him," the blonde said.

Jase walks slowly toward the sign that indicated the men's room. By the time he got there, Kostya was walking out of the handicapped stall. "This one is free," he said as he walked by Jase. Jase headed in and found Nolan standing on the toilet seat.

"Their boss is going to text these idiots fifteen minutes before we're supposed to shut off the lights," Jase whispers. "After we're done, they'll kill us."

"Naturally," Nolan drawls. "Where's Ryker?"

"He's in bad shape. Concussion. He needs to be in a hospital. Immediately. They took him in a landscaping truck. We drove in together, but when we got here, we drove to the front. They went to what I assume is the parking area."

Nolan nodded. "Do you think that the landscaping truck has something to do with the plot?"

"Yeah," Jase said. "It was a high-end private

landscape truck. Definitely could have something to do with this place."

"I'll let the others know."

"Two more things. The guy who paid for the hit on the prince, his name, is Sergei. Apparently, the prince is having an affair with his wife. Also, Brax has been made. They're going to let the woman use him until the C-4 has been recovered, then he's toast."

Nolan paled. "Good info." He reached down and flushed the toilet. He handed Jase a phone. "Keep this handy. It's on vibrate. We'll keep you informed of what's going on."

Jase nodded, and grabbed some toilet paper and shoved it into his pocket with the phone, then opened the door and stepped out.

"Come on," his blonde babysitter said.

"Gotta wash my hands first."

There was an air of expectation. The museum was at capacity. It seemed like everybody from Dubai was here to see the prince and his family. It made the job tougher to get to the doors down to the lower levels, but they made it. It was a little less than an hour before the speeches were to begin.

Because of the dry run they had previously done, they knew that the basement area near the equipment only had one employee guarding it. The man was huddled in a back corner at his desk with a television set.

Gideon explained this to their new handlers.

"Understood," the short black man said as they headed down the stairs to the equipment room.

As soon as they made their way to the equipment room floor, the black man nodded to the redhead to go in, and he told Jase and Gideon to stay in the stairwell.

The redhead came back.

"It's done. Let's go."

Fuck!

He'd killed the guy who wasn't even going to notice us.

Jase gritted his teeth and led the way to the area that housed the switchgears.

"Now we wait," the blonde man said.

Jase looked down at his watch. The speeches would start in about twenty-five minutes, and then Sergei would want the prince killed. How did the Kraken have this planned? There was a lot of green space around the highly decorative building. Since they were using the landscaping truck, they had to be using the cover of the green space to hide a sniper. There weren't any tall buildings around the museum.

Jase pictured the highly stylized eye, which made up the formation of the building, and figured out where the podium would be in front of the reflective pool. Almost anyplace in the grass, trees or bushes would provide an excellent shot to the podium. Then the prince would suffer for boinking Sergei's woman.

Jase watched as Gideon looked over at their three babysitters. Jase knew he was considering the best way to take them down.

He felt his phone vibrate.

He sneezed. Then pulled up his arm so he could sneeze into his elbow. He sneezed two more times. He twisted around to pull toilet paper out of his pocket to wipe his nose. Then read that there were supposed to be two shooters. How Kostya got that information he didn't know, but he'd take it to the bank.

He shoved the tissue and phone back into his pocket.

He huffed out a laugh. The Kraken Elite sure wanted to make sure they didn't fuck up and not earn their fifty million. How hard was it going to be to shoot one guy in the head? All Sergei wanted was to make the dude suffer, for God's sake.

Jase stopped moving. He stopped breathing. Getting yourself killed would not make you suffer.

He shut his eyes for a moment and remembered the picture he'd seen in the museum's lobby that showed the prince with his wife and three young children. Dying would not make the prince suffer. Having your wife and kids killed in front of you? Yeah, that would make you suffer.

The black guy's phone rang.

Shit, they had fifteen minutes, and they were trying to stop the wrong assassination!

Jase didn't have time to explain shit to Gideon, but he knew he'd go along with him. Jase waited until he finished his call, then he kicked the boss in the side of his knee so that it hit his other knee. The man cried out in pain and headed for the hard floor. Jase helped him by stomping his foot on the back of his skull.

As he turned, Red's fist was heading for his temple.

Jase ducked and shoved his head into Red's chin. Then he followed it up with three rabbit punches to Red's kidneys.

"Finish him," Gideon shouted.

Jase pushed him away and shot out with a roundhouse kick to the head, that dropped Ted to the floor.

"What now?" Gideon asked.

Jase pulled out the phone that Nolan had given him and keyed in Kostya's number. He only knew about four of his teammates' numbers, most of them were just on auto-dial. Kostya didn't pick up.

Fuck!

He texted back on the phone.

'Prince's family is the target.'

He waited for at least seven seconds, but there was no reply. He shoved the phone at Gideon. "The prince's family is the target, not the prince. They're going to be in the audience, right?"

"I think so."

"I got a text from Nolan saying that there are two shooters."

"Landscapers," Gideon said. He was on the right page.

"Exactly."

"Let's move," Gideon said as he started running toward the stairwell.

They hightailed it up the stairs. When they got to the lobby floor, they each took a deep breath so that they could look calm when they came out of the stairwell.

"Hold up," Gideon said as Jase went to open the

door. He was looking at the cell phone display. "They have spotted one of the shooters. They don't want to take him out until they can do it simultaneously with the other one."

"Have they spotted the other one?" Jase asked as Gideon's fingers were flying across the keys.

Gideon shook his head.

Jase yanked open the door.

There was no way they were going to get to the VIP audience to warn the prince's family. Even if they just started shooting to warn the prince's bodyguards, there was too much of a chance that the Kraken could take out one or more of the family members in the confusion. Nope, they had to take out the shooters.

The phone rang in Gideon's hands.

"Got it."

He turned to Jase. "Victor and Nolan found Ryker. He's convulsing. They're getting him to the hospital."

Jase took the phone from Gideon and looked down at his watch. "Seven minutes is when Ely expects the lights to go out."

"I hear you," Kostya responded. "Linc has a lock on one sniper. He's on the west side of the entrance. That sniper is literally in a bush. We're searching the east side now. No luck so far."

"We'll also scout the east side Jase promised. "But you're going to have to take the shot, boss. Since we were in the museum, we don't have weapons."

"Understood."

"Kostya, you can be damn sure we'll find him." Gideon promised.

Her Defiant Warrior | 221

It was dusk and the light show had started. It was gorgeous. Every color in the rainbow, and special three-dimensional effects, were all on display. Taking shots in this mess was going to take a special kind of skill.

"There is no way we can just run around on the landscaped grounds," Gideon pointed out reasonably. "That's why they were using the landscapers as a cover."

"We just need to spot them. Kostya will do the rest."

"Really? With this light show going on, you think you can spot them?"

Jase tuned out his friend. There was something he wasn't remembering. He was with the rest of the crowd, far away from the VIP area, waiting for the prince to make his way to the podium.

Think Drakos. Think.

They got jostled by a group of French tourists. They were all really excited, and if they didn't have cameras in front of their faces, they had binoculars.

Jase squeezed his eyes shut for a second. Then opened them and tried to find a good mark to steal a set of binoculars. The kid looked to be about thirteen. His binoculars were laying on the ground beside him. He had his smart phone up to his face as he took pictures. Jase swiped the binoculars and quickly melted into the crowd.

"I've got mine," Gideon whispered.

They were both taller than most of the tourists so

they could look toward the east landscaping above the entrance.

"Check out that tree. I think I see movement," Gideon pointed.

Jase looked but saw nothing. "There's nothing there," he told Gideon.

He slowly did another sweep of the vast amounts of grass, then looked at the few thin trees. So much grass.

Just how many landscapers did they employ?

And why would a landscaper *bring* grass clippings *to* a job?

Huh?

Jase thought back to the white truck he saw Ryker drive away in. Green grass clippings had fluttered out the back.

"They're hiding under grass clippings," he yelled at Gideon.

"What?"

"Trust me. Look for a lump of grass that looks a little uneven. It'll be a sniper hiding under grass clippings."

Jase got out the cell phone to report to Kostya.

15

THE MUSIC CAME TO A CRESCENDO AS THE PRINCE walked up to the dais.

Fuck. Fuck. Fuck.

Dammit, Kostya wasn't on the phone with them, he had to be on the phone with Linc. Pray God that he would find the shooter.

"I see him," Gideon yelled out. "I communicated to Kostya. Kostya has him in his sights."

"Great, now we have to find Ely." Jase yelled to Gideon over the music.

Gideon didn't miss a beat. He turned his attention to Jase. "I'll take the east. You stay on this side."

Jase nodded. Ely was as tall as Jase was. Seventy-five percent of the men were wearing a keffiyeh, so now he just had to look for a man with light brown hair and his height. He did a slow sweep with his binoculars.

Nothing.

He pushed his way through a throng of people to get a new position to look again. As the music came to an end, the prince raised his arms to hush the roaring crowd. When there was finally silence, he began to speak.

The crack of a shot ripped through the air. Most people would have heard only one shot, but Jase heard two, and he smiled.

The prince was wrestled to the ground and covered by two large bodyguards. Jase did a quick sweep of the grass on the west lawn with his binoculars. He saw a glimmer of red mist and grinned.

He immediately started looking for Ely again. But now it was tougher. The crowd was jostling one another. A voice boomed over the loud speaker.

"This is just a drill. Do not be alarmed. This is just a drill."

The words were being repeated in ten different languages and being displayed across the eye of the building. The prince and his family were long gone. Jase continued to look for Ely.

You fucking son-of-a-bitch, be on my side of the entrance.

Still nothing.

Jase made another sweep and — *There was the motherfucker.*

Jase pushed through mothers and fathers, old and young, avoiding women with babies and the elderly until he could put hands on Ely. One well planted hit to the side of his head, and Ely went down like a sack of potatoes. Jase felt the burn of the knife as it cut through into his tricep from behind.

Dammit!

He elbowed the man who'd come at him with a knife.

He heard people yelling for the police in Arabic.

Out of the corner of his eye, he saw Bull trying to pull Ely up off the ground. Jase twisted and landed a hard punch to the jaw of the man with the knife, then kicked him in the stomach. When the man doubled over, he dropped the knife. Jase picked it up, felt the grip, then threw it at Bull, where it caught the big man in his eye.

He felt another man coming up from behind, but then he was gone. When Jase turned around, he saw Kostya standing over a dead body.

"Hold it!" what seemed like over fifteen men in military uniforms surrounded them. "Get down on the ground. Hands behind your head."

Kostya and Jase immediately went down to the ground, with their hands behind their heads.

IT TOOK FIVE DAYS, five long days before Jase and Kostya actually saw blue sky again. Until that time, they were held apart from one another, in a place that had no name. The American Ambassador met them before they were ushered outside. He explained that the C-4 had been confiscated, and all the other members of Omega Sky were accounted for and had left the country four days ago. He said before they could leave the country, they needed to meet with one more person and after that, they were to leave Dubai and never return.

Kostya and Jase looked at one another in confusion as they were led to an armored limousine where they were asked to get in. They were then handed black silk bands and told to blindfold themselves. They both shrugged and did as they were told. All in all, this did not have the earmarks of an execution.

They were driven for over an hour before they were escorted out of the limousine and taken into an air-conditioned residence. When they were told to remove their blindfolds, they found themselves standing before the young prince of Dubai.

"Welcome," he said in English. "I wanted to take this time alone with you to express my gratitude."

Kostya and Jase both nodded. After all, what else was there to say or do? Up close, Jase could see just how young the prince really was.

"I cannot thank you enough for what you did for my family."

He really was a kid, and his thanks were heartfelt. Jase wanted to tell him that if he really meant it, he'd keep it in his pants from now on.

"We were happy to be of service," Kostya finally said.

"My people have told me that there is nothing I can offer you," the prince went on. "They tell me you are like my country's elite military, and you would not take any rewards. But is there not something I can do for you or offer you?"

"No, there is not. We just do our job," Kostya answered.

"And you Mr. Drakos?" The prince said as he turned to Jase.

Before Jase shook his head, he looked deep into the young kid's eyes.

"Does the name Sergei mean anything to you?" Jase asked.

Kostya shot him a hard look.

For just a brief moment, the prince looked rattled. He quickly masked it.

"The name Sergei now means nothing to anyone in the world," the prince answered.

Jase nodded with satisfaction.

"Al-salaam 'alaikum." The prince said to them solemnly.

"Peace be with you as well, sir," Jase responded.

As they flew back to the United States in first class on Emirates Airlines, Kostya looked over at Jase. "You just couldn't leave it alone, could you?"

"Nope," Jase answered.

"Good. It saved me the trouble."

16

It had only been two and a half weeks, but it had seemed like two and a half months since Bonnie had seen Jase. She'd gone over to Farah and Malik's house twice. Both times she said it was so the twins could play with Punk. Farah didn't believe her, but Malik did, so there was that, at least.

"Honey, he's going to be fine. They do this all the time, you know that, right? You went out with Jase for five weeks. You knew he was an active Navy SEAL. You knew he would be deployed on missions."

Bonnie nodded. "In theory, I knew that. In theory, I know that one day my little boy will lose his virginity and my baby girl will more than likely become a criminal mastermind. This is all well and good in theory. I did not expect this to slap me in the face."

Bonnie took a deep, shuddery breath.

I can do this.

Farah took pity on her.

"He's good at his job, honey. He's been doing this for years and years and years. He hasn't been coming home safe and sound because he's lucky. He's been coming home safe and sound because he's really good at what he does and he's got a fucking fantastic team of men surrounding him. You should really talk to some of the other women. I'm surprised you showed up here, and not at Lark or Jada's place."

"I haven't met them," Bonnie admitted.

"I'm confused. Why haven't you met them? Malik and I were invited over to one of Gideon's barbecues just before they were deployed. We couldn't make it, but Jase had to have taken you and the kids. If they love Punk, they would adore Lucy."

Bonnie bit the tip of her thumb. "I haven't wanted them to get the wrong idea and think that Jase was my boyfriend or man friend or something like that. I didn't want them to get attached and then have us break up."

Farah stood up from her kitchen table.

"Are you out of your mind? You're gone for my brother-in-law. What do you mean, break-up?"

"He's a Navy SEAL."

"And?"

"Well, they're not known for their relationship-expectancy."

"Girl, you have some messed up thoughts going on in your head. You know that? And here I just thought you were messed up about cherry pie."

"Mom, can we go with Maryanne to the swimming pool?" Lachlan asked as he rounded the corner into the kitchen.

"No, I didn't pack your swimming suits."

Amber followed her brother into the kitchen and picked a baby carrot off of the tray in front of Bonnie and swiped it into the hummus and popped it into her mouth.

"I already thought of that, Mom. Maryanne said she'd stop on by our house and we could change into our suits there."

"Honey, Maryanne is not here to be your babysitter."

"Mrs. Larkin, this gives me perfect cover. I wanted to see Charlie again, but I don't want him to think I'm going to the pool just to see him. If I go with Amber and Lachlan, then it doesn't look like I showed up to see him."

"Honey, if you go with Amber and Lachlan, all your attention has to be on them, not on Charlie." Farah pointed out.

"Exactly! I'll be ignoring him, so he'll totally be into me at school on Monday."

"Isn't she the coolest Mom? I'm learning so much." Amber was positively glowing.

"Let me give you some money for the pool. I need some more grown-up time with your Auntie Farah. Apparently, your mom needs more wisdom."

"Yay!"

Bonnie dug money out of her purse and gave it to her kids and waved them off.

"So, let me get this straight," Farah started. "You could be role-modeling a healthy male female relationship, or your kids could learn relationships from TV, the internet or worst of all, my daughter. Is that how you want to play it?"

"This is not a conversation for carrots and hummus."

"Margaritas?" Farah asked.

"Cheesecake?" Bonnie countered hopefully.

"I've got cookie dough ice cream."

"Sold."

"What the hell are you doing picking me up from the airport?" Jase said as he saw his brother at baggage claim. He gave his brother a big hug.

"I wanted to see you before you disappeared into the depths of a Little Creek debrief."

"Hey Renzo," Kostya held out his hand.

Renzo shook Jase's lieutenant's hand.

"I'd stay and talk," Kostya began, "but, I—"

"Kostya!"

All three men turned when a beautiful blonde woman came running their way. Kostya's face transformed as he smiled at his wife. He held out his arms and caught her as she jumped up into his arms.

Jase chuckled as they kissed, then turned to his brother. "There's my duffel bag. One perk of first class, my bag comes off first."

"First class?"

"Made friends with a prince, so I got a perk," Jase grinned. "Let's get going. So, tell me why you needed to talk to me. Is it the family? Angelica? The folks?"

"No, to all of the above. They're all fine. Angelica took the part, so she should be stable for the next year or so on the movie set. Nope, it's about me. I need some advice."

"Shit Renz. Out of the two of us, you're more level-headed. Malik's even more level-headed than you are. Why come to me?"

"I need advice about me. I'm not reading myself clearly, so I wanted an outsider's, who knows me, opinion." Renzo said as they crossed the bridge over to the covered parking.

Jase laughed. "That kind of makes sense, in a teenage girl's way of thinking. Hit me with it."

"I have loved traveling around. I've loved it. I take after dad. Taking on different projects, traveling the world and building things has made me happy."

Jase nodded. "We all know that."

"Do you ever think I could do something else? Do you think I could be happy staying in one place?"

"I'm thirty-seven. That means you're thirty-five. You've lived most of your life as a rolling stone. I've got a question for you. Have you ever been bored? Tired? Lonely?"

"Well sure. That's when I come home and see all of you." Renzo unlocked the rental with his key fob.

"It used to be, we wouldn't see you for a year or two. Now we see you every six months. What does that tell you?"

They got into the Chevy Malibu.

Renzo didn't say anything as they drove out of the

airport. Jase knew his brother. He liked to process in silence.

"Do you own your own car?" Jase finally asked.

"When I'm on a big job, I'll get a truck while I'm there. Nothing special."

"Then you'll get a glamourous car like this when you're here in town. Must be nice," Jase teased.

Renzo gave him the side-eye.

"So, what's this conversation really about?" Jase asked.

"You know I spent time in Jasper Creek, Tennessee, right?"

"Yep."

"It's a small town. It felt good. It felt right."

"It's pretty far from all of us," Jase pointed out.

"Yeah, but it's where Millie's farm is at."

"Millie, huh?"

"Yeah. Millie. And I don't want to start something, if I'm just going to end up being some asshole who's a rolling stone and destined to leave."

"Renzo, you don't have it in yourself to be an asshole. Not to the right woman. Now tell me all about her."

TWO DAYS OF DEBRIEFING. It might not have been as long as they had him in solitary in Dubai, but it felt even longer because he was so close to Bonnie. All the others, but Kostya, had already been home for days.

He'd seen their group texts as soon as he got his personal cell phone returned to him after the debrief was done. The Navy didn't mess around; they wanted to make sure that everything matched up. Especially when there was a rogue CIA agent involved.

Captain Hale had talked to him for twenty minutes. He wanted to ensure that if the prince or anyone from the UAE ever reached out to him, that he would immediately report it to Kostya. Jase hadn't really considered that might happen. But, all things considered, the Captain might be onto something, so Jase promised.

The first thing he wanted to do when he left base was call Bonnie, but first he needed to get cleaned up. A shower sounded wonderful, and he was hoping more of his absorbable stitches might have fallen out, and maybe they would if he accidentally scrubbed too hard in the shower. He really didn't want Bonnie to see him injured.

When he pulled up to his house, he saw something taped on his front door. What UPS delivery had he missed while he was gone? He hit the remote to his garage door and pulled in.

"Shower here I come."

When he was done with the shower, he took time to give himself a smooth shave. He'd been feeling itchy for days. All but one of his absorbable stitches had fallen out in the shower, so he used his tweezers to pluck out the last little tricky one. He pulled on a pair of sweat shorts and headed for the kitchen. Once again, he found the kitchen pretty well empty. But he did a frozen pretzel which he nuked. He ate it with some hot mustard and apple juice.

He looked at the clock over his stove and saw it was almost noon.

It's Wednesday. Bonnie clocks out early on Wednesdays.

Jase marched down his hallway to his bedroom and got dressed in double time. He grabbed his keys and his phone and headed for his Mustang. As soon as he got on the road to the salon, he called Farah's number.

"Jase!" she shouted. "You're home!"

"Softer, sweetheart. You're worse than artillery training."

"You're home," she whispered.

"I am," he agreed. "Look, sweetheart, I need a favor. Do you know where Lachlan and Amber go to school?"

"Sure, I do."

"Can you pick them up for me? I want to surprise Bonnie at the salon today and take her out to dinner."

"Bullshit. You want to take her somewhere horizontal," Farah laughed.

"Okay, maybe we order dinner in. Anyway, can you pick them up for me?"

"You are so in luck. I do know where they go to school, and I'm one of the people who can pick them up. I'll bring them over to my house and they get to have Tacos a la Drakos."

"Great."

"You're also in luck, because today is one of Bonnie's short days. She usually gets off work at one and does her errands. If you move your cute little tushie, you should be able to catch her before she leaves."

"I know that. Why do you think I'm going ten over the speed limit? Thanks for picking up the kids. You're a doll."

"I know," Farah laughed.

17

"I need to take it down."

"Okay. I've got to tell you. You are now, officially, on my last nerve," Shannon said.

Bonnie looked at her watch again.

Twelve-forty-five.

She closed up her station and took out her purse. Why in the hell was she waiting? It wasn't as if she were really on the clock. If another walk-in came in, there were two other stylists who could take them. She needed to get over to Jase's house in case he came home tonight or tomorrow.

She'd almost all but said she loved him, for God's sake.
In a note!
Like she was in junior high school!

"Bonnie Fiona Larkin, don't you dare go over to that man's house!" Shannon shouted as she continued to spray hairspray on her client. She bent down and patted the woman on her shoulder. "I'll be right back."

Shannon ran as fast as she could in four-inch heels.

She caught up to Bonnie in the front lobby of the salon. "You did the right thing. You had been going back and forth on the relationship thing with that nice, sweet and hot as fuck man, for weeks. You finally took a stand by writing him a letter, which he probably isn't going to see for a while. You've made up your mind to send him a letter a week until he gets home. And now you're thinking about wimping out. No way, no, sir. Not on my watch."

"It's not just that I said I liked him, Shannon. I sounded like a junior high school dork. He's going to read the note and dump me. It's going to be horrible." She walked right up to Shannon and whispered in her face. "He'll laugh at me."

"What are you talking about, honey?"

Bonnie spun around.

"Jase?"

"In the flesh," he smiled.

"You didn't read the note," she grinned. "Thank God."

"Honey, what are you talking about?"

Then Bonnie pulled her head out of her ass. "Oh my God," she screeched. "You're home!" She ran the three feet that it took to get to him, then jumped up into his arms. "Jase! You're home!"

"I am." He grinned down at her.

She pulled on his neck and he bent down. She lifted her face up and he kissed her. It was a miracle kiss where everything that was off kilter in her world, spun around and then locked exactly into its correct place.

He was holding her close by clutching her ass, and she had her legs clamped around his hips. The kiss was deep, wet and wonderful.

"Is he a Navy SEAL?" a woman asked loudly.

"Yes, he is," Shannon answered.

"How did she get him to go out with her?" the woman asked.

Jase lifted his head. "Come on Bonnie. Let's take this show on the road."

He looked so good she could barely stand it.

"You with me? You want to go?"

She nodded.

He set her down, and she stumbled as her feet hit the ground. He put his arm around her waist and she leaned her head against his shoulder. They headed for the front door.

"Hold up. She dropped this." Shannon handed Jase her purse.

They walked down the stairs to the front parking lot. "I'd normally suggest you follow me home, but I think we'll leave your car here, and I'll drive you to my house. We'll pick up your car later."

"S'okay." Bonnie gave him a dazed smile.

Jase is home!

He got the door to his Mustang open and tucked her in and buckled the seatbelt.

"Are you okay, honey?" he asked.

Bonnie looked up at him. Then shook her head. She took a deep breath and felt her eyes burn. "I'm fine. Now that you're home, I'm great."

He leaned in and gave her a lingering kiss. "I'm glad

you're great," he whispered. She watched as he got in and started the car.

"I have a confession to make," Jase said as they pulled out into traffic.

Bonnie braced. "Okay. Hit me with it."

His head whipped around. "Honey. Calm. It's me. I'm just boring old Jase Drakos. Nothing bad, I promise. My confession is that I arranged to have Farah pick up your kids so we could have more time together today."

Bonnie relaxed back into her seat.

They were quiet as he maneuvered through traffic towards his house.

"In my defense, there is nothing boring about you. I have how many more of your siblings to meet?"

"Ten, I think."

"You're what they call a special operator, right?"

"Yeah."

"Therefore, not boring."

"Yeah, but in real life. For me, my priorities are family, friends, good food and a decent-sized TV."

"I'm all about good food, but shouldn't God and country be up there before a decent-sized TV?"

"God and country are a given, babe."

JASE OPENED the door to the kitchen and followed Bonnie in. Who was this woman? What happened to the confident, take-charge woman he was used to? He watched as she immediately went to the black granite countertop and dragged her finger over the top. Then she looked at the white cabinetry. "I would have never picked out the black and white combination, but it's gorgeous."

"I didn't pick it out. I was overseas. I told Malik and Farah my price range and that I wanted to live close to them, and they arranged this."

Her eyes got wide. "You trusted them to buy your house?"

"Absolutely. I wanted a good investment, which I knew Malik would have covered, then I wanted something that would be big enough to have the family over, which I knew Farah would ensure. I also wanted something that my parents could come and stay for a bit and maybe someday it could morph into a family home." Bonnie was now next to the sink in the kitchen, and Jase moved beside her.

"When did you buy this house?"

"Three years ago."

"You weren't kidding me; you really have been looking for something permanent in your life."

"Yeah, I have," he admitted. "I would never have gotten so involved with you, a mother with two young children, if I wasn't interested in something permanent. But that's not to say I was positive where this would lead." He turned and cornered her.

"Neither was I," Bonnie admitted.

"But I'm pretty damn sure now."

"Kiss me?" she asked.

"Always. I always want to kiss you. I always want to talk to you. I always want to be near you."

"You do?"

How can she sound so surprised?

Jase tugged at the clip that kept her hair up and watched as all those beautiful curls cascaded down around her face and shoulders. He pushed her hair back from the nape of her neck so he could place a soft kiss right behind her ear.

Bonnie shuddered. He kissed her again, this time allowing his tongue to touch her soft pearly skin, tasting a smile, a memory, a wish. Bonnie trembled and pressed her body closer to his, her small, yet mighty fingers digging into his forearms. He trailed kisses along her jaw until he felt the heat of her panting breath, and she was his.

He slid his fingers through her hair, holding her in place for the ultimate taste. The hot, welcoming kiss at the salon was fine, but this was a kiss for a connoisseur. Bonnie had the prettiest lips. She didn't wear lipstick, but she was constantly putting on flavored lip gloss, and bubblegum was his favorite. Lucky him, it was today's flavor.

He breathed in through his mouth, savoring the sugary goodness, then he licked her bottom lip and she melted against him. Having her mold her curves against the hard planes of his body made him rejoice. He twisted, so he was leaning against the counter, his legs parted, and Bonnie draped across him.

He licked her top lip, and more sweetness exploded on his tongue, shooting through his body, coalescing in his cock. Bonnie's stomach was resting against his crotch, and he didn't know if she was aware of the way she was writhing against his erection or not, but please God, don't let her stop.

Jase tilted her head just a little, so when he thrust his tongue inside the molten heat of her mouth, it was a perfect fit. Bonnie must have thought so too, because she welcomed him in, sucking, scraping, dancing, beguiling him to stay and play. Jase didn't know who was the kisser and who was the kissee. All he knew was that he was drowning in the taste and torment of Bonnie Larkin.

When her nails bit into his pectoral muscle it was then he realized he was gripping her ass. When in the hell had that happened? He twirled them around and made sure that Bonnie had the softest landing possible on his granite countertop. Then he pulled off her shoes and socks, and unfastened her slacks, sliding them down along with her panties.

"Jase."

There was no fear. No confusion. Not in the way she said his name. Only the sound of satisfaction.

"Spread your legs for me, Baby," he breathed. He watched her wanton expression and her siren's smile. He couldn't take his eyes off her face. Then he caught another scent besides bubblegum. It was something even more alluring.

Jase looked down to see the prettiest pussy he had ever seen in his life. The core of his woman was open before him. Her need was glistening. No, not just glistening, he actually saw her pulse liquid fire and he couldn't wait another second.

Jase used the tip of his thumb to gather up her cream and sucked the tangy essence off his thumb.

"So good," he groaned.

Bonnie bit her lower lip, and Jase could see a blush bloom on her chest and begin to sweep up her neck. "Don't be shy now, honey. We're just getting to the good stuff."

"O-O-Okay?"

Jase chuckled at her stutter, then used his thumbs to gently part her folds and licked her gorgeous pussy. Now he felt like *he* was in a daze. Getting to taste and savor, but at the same time, feel Bonnie wiggle, shiver, moan and sigh was like getting to eat dessert before eating your dessert for dinner. It was the best of every world.

When she wiggled too much, he moved one hand and splayed it over her stomach to keep her in place, then speared his tongue deep inside her core in punishment? Or was that a reward? Who knew? Who cared?

Jase reluctantly gave up the taste of her to torture her some more. He pierced her with two fingers, then sucked her clitoris...hard.

"Jase," she screamed.

I like that.

This time he nibbled her clit and she started to chant his name as he gently moved his fingers until she jerked wildly.

Found it!

He caressed her G-spot as he sucked her clit.

Again.

Again.

Again.

"Jase!"

Her hips careened upwards, as she screamed out, her orgasm taking over. He moved his arm fast, and when her ass dropped back down, she landed on his hand, not hard granite.

Jase picked her up and cradled her against his chest. It took long minutes for Bonnie to catch her breath.

"I really like your kitchen," she said. "Now I want to tour your bedroom."

Jase laughed.

"You paid for the food online, I want to give the delivery guy an extra tip," Bonnie insisted.

"Bonnie, there's not a chance in hell that I'm going to let you open my front door to some stranger after dark. That's just not happening."

Jase went to the front door and tipped the pizza delivery girl an extra ten and took the two pizzas, wings and brownies from her. He also grabbed the UPS notice off the front of the door and brought it all to the dining room table.

"You know, we haven't christened your dining room table yet," Bonnie purred.

"First food, then christening," Jase smiled. "But I got to tell you, I love your enthusiasm. He looked over at the woman who was walking around in his T-shirt and grinned. She was absolutely perfect. Except for liking pineapple on her pizza.

"Why don't you get the plates and the silver wear, and I'll get everything opened up?" she suggested.

"Sounds good."

Jase headed to the kitchen and set down the notice next to the other stuff that he needed to go through later. That's when he noticed it wasn't a UPS notice. It was an envelope with his name written on it with a woman's curly script.

"What the hell?"

He ripped it open.

"How about before you read that, I name a couple of sexual acts that we haven't tried out yet, and you choose one? And in return, you don't read the letter?" Bonnie asked hopefully as she entered the kitchen.

Jase looked down at the letter and read Bonnie's name at the bottom.

"Is this a 'Dear John' letter?" Jase asked her.

"Not even close."

"Then why can't I read it?" he asked.

"Because I sound like I'm in junior high school, and I kind of want you to think better of me."

Jase watched as she bit the end of her thumb.

"Junior high, huh? What did you look like in junior high? I bet you were cute."

"This isn't funny. Can you just give me the letter?"

He looked down at it one more time, then he read how she ended it and barked out a laugh. "Uhm, no. There is no way that I'm not going to read this whole damn letter," he said as he continued to chuckle.

He watched as she put her fingers in her ears.

"Why are you doing that?" he asked.

"So, I can't hear you laugh."

"You just heard me ask why you're doing that," he pointed out reasonably.

She covered her eyes with both hands. "Fine. Read the damned letter. Our pizza's getting cold."

Jase looked down at the pretty purple paper and started reading.

Jase,

I've been missing you a lot. I know you told me that you wouldn't know how long you would be gone, so I've decided to write you a letter each week, just to keep you up to date on the Larkin family happenings.

Maryanne took Lachlan and Amber to the pool yesterday. That niece of yours is something else. She sure is playing the long game with this boy named Charlie. I don't think you ever have to worry about some boy doing her wrong. The boys will all be playing checkers while she's playing three-dimensional chess. The only thing that has me worried is that Amber is learning at her knee.

Meanwhile, Farah told me that there is a dog named Lucy that the kids would love to meet. I had to come clean with her that I've passed on meeting some of your friends, and I'm so sorry about that. I really do want to meet your friends, and I want my kids to meet your friends and more of your family.

Besides telling you about all of our 'goings-on' I thought I might talk about feelings. Those aren't my best things in the world. Okay, maybe they're my worst thing in the world. I'm great at feelings when I share them with my kids. I want Amber and Lachlan to grow up knowing they are the most wonderful and loved human beings on planet earth. I think the little hooligans have figured out that they have me wrapped around their little fingers. But you, Jase Drakos, you have me tied up in knots. In a good way, not a bad way.

So, this is letter number one. I'll be mailing the rest. Farah told me not to be worried about you because you kick-ass, but I'll tell you a secret. I'm a little bit worried about you. So, I'm saying a prayer for you every night before I go to sleep, and every morning before I get out of bed.

STAY SAFE, *Jase.*

ALL MY LIKE,
 Bonnie

18

He looked up front the paper in his hand and stared at the woman in front of him. He reached over and gently pried her hands away from her eyes. "Why didn't you want me to read this, Bonnie?"

She bit her bottom lip and winced. "Because I basically say I love you, without actually saying it?" she squeaked out the question.

"Are you sure that's the reason you didn't want me to read it?" Jase asked as he stroked his fingers around the neckline of the t-shirt she was wearing.

"Let me think." She put her index finger to her chin. Looked down. Then back up at him. "Yep. That's why."

Jase chuckled.

"Family, your sense of humor, friends, good food, a decent-sized TV. That's my new list of priorities."

"I'm kind of a goof," she warned.

"Come let's eat pizza, goofy girl. Then you have to go pick up your children from Farah and Malik's."

"Sounds good."

"How'd it go?" Jase asked.

They'd agreed Bonnie would tell her kids over the weekend that they were dating. He'd been chomping at the bit to find out what their response had been. He was pretty sure it would be fine, but you never knew. After all, he'd be the first boyfriend their mother had ever had.

"They took it well. Really well. They do have some questions, though."

"Like what?"

"Nothing bad. But they would love it if you could come over tonight."

"Shit Bonnie, I can't. We're training for the next three days."

"Can you come over on Saturday?"

"What time?" Jase asked.

"Five-thirty. I know that's early, but it gives them time to do their homework and still have screen time before they go to bed."

"Honey, five-thirty is good for me," Jase assured her.

"Bring a change of clothes. I also told them that sometimes you and I would have sleepovers."

"You jumped in with both feet, huh?"

"No point in waiting," she chuckled.

"I'll see you at five-thirty. Is there anything I can bring?"

"Nope, we're covered," she assured him.

Her Defiant Warrior | 253

JASE SHOWED up five minutes early. He brought a Teeter Cherry Pie for Lachlan and Bonnie, and three different flavors of ice cream. One of them had to be to Amber's liking. Before he could knock on the door, Lachlan had it open.

"You need to use the peephole, kid," Jase admonished.

"Nope, got a sweet system set up," Lachlan said as he held up his mother's smart phone. "I heard someone on the step, and I could see you through the peephole on mom's phone. Looking out a peephole is for old people."

Jake sighed. "I'm an old person," he admitted as he handed Lachlan the pie box.

"Mom! Your boyfriend brought me Teeter Pie. Sure hope he brought something for you."

Amber came running out from down the hall. She eyed the Harris Teeter grocery bag. "Did you get something for you and me, Jase?"

"You like ice cream, right?"

"Depends. What flavor?"

"Chocolate chip mint. Cookie Dough and since I also bought vanilla, I brought chocolate syrup too."

Amber gave him a huge grin that looked so much like her mother's he would do anything for her. Hell, she could tell him to go back to the store and get strawberry ice cream, and he'd do it.

"Mom.," she yelled into the kitchen. "He's a keeper. He brought chocolate syrup to go with the ice cream." Amber took the bags from him. "Why don't you sit down on the sofa? There's a game starting soon. I'm sure you don't want to miss it. I'll bring you a beer."

She left like a shot and was soon back with the promised beer.

Oh shit, she's setting me up.

"Amber, are you okay with your mom and me dating?" he asked cautiously.

"I'm loving it. It totally gives you street cred if your mom is dating a SEAL. Maryanne told me to tell people at school. She and her sisters always mentioned you, and nobody ever gave them trouble. So, I'll start doing the same thing."

"Is somebody causing you trouble?" he asked.

"Not me. Lachlan and I are a team, so people don't mess with the two of us."

Jase didn't doubt that. But if it wasn't him dating her mother and it wasn't school, what was all the buttering up about?

"You know you can talk to your mom about anything, right?" Jase asked.

"She was contra...contradicking herself. So, since this is about you, I decided to just go to the source, and ask."

"Okay, ask," Jase smiled.

I'm rocking this boyfriend gig.

"My softball team needs a coach. I told the girls I knew someone who would be perfect."

"What happened to your old coach?"

"He got a job in Utah and had to move. Which is good because he always put his daughter in as first base, but she could never catch the ball. So can you do it?"

"You want me to be your team's coach?" Jase repeated the question to give himself more time to think.

Amber nodded.

Jase turned off the TV and waved her to the chair that was kitty-corner to the couch. "Amber, I have a job that requires some traveling. I'm not sure I could always make it to the practices and games."

"I told them you were a Navy SEAL and would have to be called out on missions sometimes. All they cared about was that you made it so I could hit the ball. Mrs. Schwartz is our assistant coach. She helps out when absolutely nobody else can be there. So, if you're on a secret mission, she can always look in your book and follow the instructions."

Ah shit.

"Honey, you're not supposed to tell people what I do for a living," he told her.

"It's okay. Remy's dad and Kirk's dad are both Navy SEAL's too."

Ah shit.

"Horace's dad is Navy SEAL support. He got injured. His leg is all fucked up so he's not out in the field anymore, but Horace likes having him home more."

Ah shit.

"Amber Lee Larkin! What did I tell you about not doing an end-run around me to get to Jase?"

"That I'm not supposed to do it."

"What else did I tell you?"

"Don't try to compliment him into doing something he doesn't want to do."

"And, what else?"

"Don't try bribing him, neither."

"And what else?"

"No flirting."

"That's my girl."

Jase burst out laughing. It was either that or cry. The brass always worried about the wives gabbing too much, and instead it was the seven-year-olds.

"I'll talk to Mrs. Schwartz."

"My kids adore you."

"I adore your kids. Actually, adore might not be the right word," Jase said as he watched Bonnie walk from the bathroom toward the queen-sized bed.

"What's the right word?"

"Adore is half the equation. The other half is that I live in fear. God forbid I screw up with you. I don't know what kind of retribution Amber will take, but it will be bad. Very, very, bad."

Bonnie giggled.

She slipped under the covers and turned off the lamp on her nightstand. Then she snuggled really close. "My advice to you is, screw up while she's young, and her powers aren't fully formed." Her hands speared through his chest hair and his breath caught. He was done talking about her children.

"Your baby doll nightgown is gorgeous, but it has to go."

Bonnie lifted her arms as he drew it over her head. She was nude underneath. Jase pulled her close and kissed her. How could he not?

"Turn out your lamp," she said.

"Why? You locked your door, didn't you?"

Bonnie nodded.

"Then the lamp stays on. I love looking at you."

Bonnie's nails dug deep into the skin of his chest. "I like looking at you, too."

Jase pushed back the hair from her face. "Bonnie, I have a serious question."

"O-o-okay."

"Do I have all your like?"

She shoved at his chest. Hard. But she was laughing.

"Yes, you have all of my like. Am I ever going to hear the end of that?"

"Nope."

19

Bonnie watched in horrified fascination as the huge black dog played tug-of-war with a long piece of rope with her two children. The dog, Lucy, suddenly let go. Amber and Lachlan ended up on their butts, laughing hysterically.

"Your kids couldn't be any cuter," Jada said as she sat down next to Bonnie. Jada Harlowe was Gideon Smith's girlfriend.

"She's right. Can I adopt them?" Lark Barona asked, as she sat down on the other side of Bonnie.

It was the second time she had met these two ladies, and already Bonnie was feeling a strong bond with them, and not just because their men all worked together.

"I'll tell you what, Lark. You are so allowed to adopt them over a weekend some time."

"Deal." Lark thrust out her hand.

"Sweet," Bonnie grinned as she shook her hand. "I get free babysitting."

"And extra sexy time with Jase Drakos. Don't forget that part of the equation," Jada reminded her.

"How could I forget?"

"How many of his siblings have you met?" Lark asked.

"Malik, Gustavo, Ronnie, Kato, Amadi and Celeste all live in this area, so I've met them. I met Renzo and Angelica the first time I met Jase. Eleni is due for a visit along with his parents in two weeks, so that will put me up to nine, that'll leave me with seven more."

"I don't know how his parents did it."

"They're still doing it," Bonnie reminded them. "They have two girls still in college."

"I forgot," Lark said.

"I'm really looking forward to meeting Eleni and her tribe. Then there's Bruno. Apparently, Jase, Bruno, Malik and Renzo were all thicker than thieves growing up."

"Can I get you ladies anything?" Kostya asked as he wandered over from the grill.

Lark held up her empty soda bottle. "Another, if you wouldn't mind, kind sir."

"You've got it. And for you all?"

"I'm good," Bonnie answered.

"Me too," Jada responded.

"Mom! Mom! Did you see?" Lachlan raced up to her and flopped down at her feet. "Lucy is a Bore mouth."

"Behemoth," Amber corrected her brother. "It means he's huge."

"Why didn't you just say he was huge?" Lachlan complained.

"Because you need to expand your vocabulary." Amber looked past Bonnie at the table and found a tortilla chip she dipped in salsa and then popped into her mouth.

"Mom, I need a smartphone so I can take notes," Amber said.

"I can buy you a small pad of paper and a pencil," Bonnie offered.

"Why do you need to take notes?" Jada asked.

"Every time I'm around Jase, I have to create another org chart to keep everybody straight. I thought his family was bad, but all of his team members are a whole other pot of fish."

"Kettle of fish," Bonnie corrected.

"Yeah, that." She turned around. "Hey Lachlan. Lucy has the rope in her mouth again. Let's go."

"Oh my God, you so have your hands full with your daughter," Lark laughed. Her eyes were sparkling.

"I'd wondered how Jase ended up coaching little girls' softball. Now I know," Jada smiled.

"Don't try to get out of babysitting," Bonnie looked at Lark. "Just because you've figured out my daughter is an evil genius, doesn't get you out of your promise."

"Not on your life. It'll just prepare us for one of our own."

JASE FELT a bone deep sense of satisfaction having Bonnie and her kids staying at his house. He was glad he'd had the fourth bedroom made up with twin beds and two little desks. They'd been so excited they had their own little 'place' at his house. He didn't expect this to last for long. Soon he'd arrange for them to have their own separate rooms, or he would just buy a bigger house. Bonnie had let it slip once that she'd always wanted a bigger family, and God knew he loved the idea of a large family. He thrived on chaos.

He pulled Bonnie closer into his arms. He loved listening to her just breathing. Doing what he did for a living... Well. It meant that you never took for granted the little things. Like having your lover sleeping in your arms. But he wanted her to be more than just a lover or a girlfriend. He wanted a wife.

She might have started out worried about his level of commitment, but he knew that his 'All my Like', girl was the one who still was holding a little piece of herself back. He was just waiting for that last wall to drop.

"Jase?"

"Go back to sleep."

"Can't." She kissed him. Right over his heart.

"Tomorrow is day camp for the kids. You have to be up early," Jase reminded her.

"This can't wait," Bonnie said as she crawled up his body, her lips now hovering over his. He could see her blue eyes sparkling in the weak dawn light. She was his everything.

He cupped the back of her head and brought her mouth down to his. She melted into his kiss. Jase rolled them over, so that he was on top. He loved the fact that she was now on birth control and they had dispensed with condoms.

He moved lower down her body.

"No! I don't want foreplay this morning. I woke up in your arms, primed. I need you inside me, Jase."

He trailed his fingers down her body and found her wet and wanting. His woman was telling the truth. She was as soft as he was hard. He drew her leg up over his hip and positioned himself at her tender entrance.

That first slide into her tight, hot depths got to him. Each and every time. Each time Jase thought his head might explode, but then he'd get himself together and start a rhythm to bring them both pleasure.

"Jase, you'll never know. You can never know. Just how much I love you."

He frowned. He loved the words, but what brought them on? Was she all right? He studied her face as his body danced with hers.

She was looking at him with her heart in her eyes. This morning wasn't just a passionate foray, there was a look of absolute trust and love in her eyes. It humbled him. Jase would do everything in his power to be the man she needed him to be.

Bonnie might not realize it yet, but Jase did. She was offering up her life and the lives of her children into his keeping, and he would never break that trust.

He thrust deep and she caught fire.

"Ahhhhh." He muffled her cry of release with a kiss. Then he fell into the stars right along with her.

At last, he had her whole heart. When he could breathe again, he told her his truth.

"I'll love you until forever ends."

EPILOGUE
3 MONTHS LATER - HAWAII

"Why'd you make us come in from the beach? Mom isn't going to be home for a whole 'nother hour. I don't know why anyone would want to take so long having someone else wash their face for them," Lachlan complained.

"Fair point," Jase nodded.

"She's also getting a massage and her toes painted." Amber explained.

There's my girl, always having her mom's back.

"Lachlan, I called you in early, because I needed to talk to you about something. Why don't you both go sit on the couch?" Jase pointed to the spot across from where he was sitting on the coffee table.

"What do you want to talk about?" Amber asked suspiciously as she climbed up to sit next to her brother.

Lachlan pushed at his sister's shoulder. "It could be good. Maybe he wants to get us a dog, so shut up."

"If I did want to get you a dog, I would talk to your

mom first, to make sure she was okay with the idea. It's important that everyone agrees with something before someone else makes a decision."

"I never agreed with an eight-thirty bed-time." Lachlan pointed out.

"I don't see that one changing, Lach." Amber sounded seventeen or thirty-seven, certainly not seven years old. "We've got to push for something more 'tainable, like a dog." She turned to Jase. "Can you talk to mom about us having a dog?"

Why am I not surprised this conversation went way off course?

"I need to talk to you two about something else before I can talk to your mom about a dog. I need your agreement before she and I can make any decisions about dogs."

Lachlan and Amber both turned to look at one another.

"Like what decisions?" Amber asked Jase carefully.

He slid down off the coffee table and got on his knees in front of the kids. He pulled the black jeweler's box out of his pocket and opened it up.

"Is it for mom?" Lachlan asked. "How much did it cost?"

Amber punched her brother in the shoulder. "Of course it's for mom." Her tiny finger reached out and touched the marquis sapphire. "It looks like Mama's eyes," she breathed out. "What's it called?"

"It's a sapphire," Jase told her.

"Oh." She pulled her hand away and sat back up on the couch, her bottom lip trembling. "Oh," she said again. Jase watched in horror as Amber's eyes filled with tears.

"Baby. What's wrong?" Jase dropped the box on the floor and reached for the little girl who owned such a big piece of his heart. "Tell me what's wrong and I'll fix it."

"It's not a diamond," she said. Now she was crying. She started to scramble off the sofa, and it wasn't towards him, it was away from him.

That was a no go.

"There are diamonds on the ring." He sounded desperate.

"But not the big one," she sobbed. "I thought you wanted to marry Mom."

"I do baby girl. I want to marry her more than almost anything in the world." He finally had her trembling body in his arms.

"Then why didn't you buy her a diamond ring?"

"I wanted to buy her a ring that would fill her with joy each and every day when she saw it. That's why I got this sapphire. It's the color of your and Lachlan's eyes. It is an engagement ring, I promise. I do want to ask your mama to marry me."

"You do?" Lachlan said as he pushed in to wipe at Amber's tears.

"I want to marry all of you. I want all of you for my family."

Amber sucked in a deep breath and then held it for so long that Jase was afraid she'd pass out. Lachlan just stared at him. Then he poked his sister in her stomach. "Breathe Amber."

A swoosh of air left Amber's mouth. "I want all of us to be married too," she said shyly. "I want us to be a family."

Lachlan looked up at Jase. His eyes were solemn, his arms were crossed over his chest. "I've seen some dads I don't like. They're not like Mr. Drakos."

Jase frowned.

"I mean the other Mr. Drakos. Your brother. I like him. He always makes Mrs. Drakos laugh. He hugs her and smiles at her. He even does it when he doesn't think anyone can see him. Kenny's dad is a jerk to his mom. Nobody can be a jerk to my mom."

Lachlan's eyes glittered blue fire at him.

Holy hell, I didn't see this coming.

"You do know that Malik and I were both raised by Grandpa Christos, right?"

Lachlan jerked his chin up in acknowledgement.

"Grandpa Christos is like Malik. He loves Grandma Sharon with his whole heart and every day he hugs her and makes her smile. He raised all of his sons, not just Malik, but me, Renzo, Gustavo, Kato, Amadi, Bruno, Ronnie, Daw and Narong all to treat the women in their lives the same way. If we didn't, he would be very disappointed in us."

"My mom is special," Lachlan told him something that he already knew.

"I will treat her like a princess," Jase promised.

He watched as Lachlan processed his words. "All right."

Amber scooched off the sofa and picked up the ring box from the floor. "Ooooh, it does have diamonds!"

"Hello. I'm back. Did you miss me?"

Jase looked up and saw Bonnie come through the doorway of their rented condo. She looked gorgeous and refreshed in her red sundress. He couldn't wait to get her alone tonight to propose.

"Jase is marrying all of us, and he's going to treat you like a princess, otherwise Grandpa Christos is going to be disappointed," Lachlan said as he bounded off the couch to give his mom a hug.

"Yeah, and you can't be disappointed in the ring, because there are some diamonds on it, so it really is an engagement ring. See?"

Amber had the ring box in her hand and was shoving it into Bonnie's for her to look at. He saw Bonnie's look of befuddlement, but then she looked over her two terrors and zeroed in on Jase. Her head tilted in question.

Jase shrugged. Of course things went wonky, it was the Larkin way.

Jase got up off the coffee table where he had been sitting and wrapped his arms around his little family.

She reached up around her children and kissed the hollow of Jase's throat. Then she whispered in his ear. "I like you very much."

"You have all my like, too." He whispered back.

She giggled.

He stroked his fingers through her hair and bit the lobe of her ear. Then he whispered. "Bonnie Fiona Larkin. You and your children have brought color into my life. Will you marry me?"

She didn't answer immediately. She was pondering,

just like her son did. Then she smiled and stood on her toes to whisper in his ear.

"Jase, I have never felt so treasured in my entire life. I don't know if I can do it, but I'll spend the rest of my life trying to show you just how much I really *do* love you. You are the piece of my heart I never knew I was missing. Yes, I will marry you, Jase Drakos. Absolutely yes."

"She said yes," Lachlan whispered loudly.

"I know. You know what that means," Amber whispered back just as loud.

"We can get a dog!" Lachlan yelled.

"We can get a baby sister!" Amber screeched.

If you want to read about Renzo and Millie, check out their book in the Protector's of Jasper Creek Series, "Her Hidden Smile." You won't want to miss it.

Don't Miss Jonas Wulff's story, Click Here!

ABOUT THE AUTHOR

Caitlyn O'Leary is a USA Bestselling Author, #1 Amazon Bestselling Author and a Golden Quill Recipient from Book Viral in 2015. Hampered with a mild form of dyslexia she began memorizing books at an early age until her grandmother, the English teacher, took the time to teach her to read -- then she never stopped. She began re-writing alternate endings for her Trixie Belden books into happily-ever-afters with Trixie's platonic friend Jim. When she was home with pneumonia at twelve, she read the entire set of World Book Encyclopedias -- a little more challenging to end those happily.

Caitlyn loves writing about Alpha males with strong heroines who keep the men on their toes. There is plenty of action, suspense and humor in her books. She is never shy about tackling some of today's tough and relevant issues.

In addition to being an award-winning author of romantic suspense novels, she is a devoted aunt, an avid reader, a former corporate executive for a Fortune 100 company, and totally in love with her husband of soon-to-be twenty years.

She recently moved back home to the Pacific Northwest from Southern California. She is so happy to see the seasons again; rain, rain and more rain. She has a large fan group on Facebook and through her e-mail list. Caitlyn is known for telling her "Caitlyn Factors", where she relates her little and big life's screw-ups. The list is long. She loves hearing and connecting with her fans on a daily basis.

Keep up with Caitlyn O'Leary:

Website: www.caitlynoleary.com
FB Reader Group: http://bit.ly/2NUZVjF
Email: caitlyn@caitlynoleary.com
Newsletter: http://bit.ly/1WIhRup

- facebook.com/Caitlyn-OLeary-Author-638771522866740
- x.com/CaitlynOLearyNA
- instagram.com/caitlynoleary_author
- amazon.com/author/caitlynoleary
- bookbub.com/authors/caitlyn-o-leary
- goodreads.com/CaitlynOLeary
- pinterest.com/caitlynoleary35

ALSO BY CAITLYN O'LEARY

PROTECTORS OF JASPER CREEK SERIES
His Wounded Heart (Book 1)
Her Hidden Smile (Book 2)

OMEGA SKY SERIES
Her Selfless Warrior (Book #1)
Her Unflinching Warrior (Book #2)
Her Wild Warrior (Book #3)
Her Fearless Warrior (Book 4)
Her Defiant Warrior (Book 5)
Her Brave Warrior (Book 6)
Her Eternal Warrior (Book 7)

NIGHT STORM SERIES
Her Ruthless Protector (Book #1)
Her Tempting Protector (Book #2)
Her Chosen Protector (Book #3)
Her Intense Protector (Book #4)
Her Sensual Protector (Book #5)
Her Faithful Protector (Book #6)
Her Noble Protector (Book #7)

Her Righteous Protector (Book #8)

NIGHT STORM LEGACY SERIES
Lawson & Jill (Book 1)

BLACK DAWN SERIES
Her Steadfast Hero (Book #1)

Her Devoted Hero (Book #2)

Her Passionate Hero (Book #3)

Her Wicked Hero (Book #4)

Her Guarded Hero (Book #5)

Her Captivated Hero (Book #6)

Her Honorable Hero (Book #7)

Her Loving Hero (Book #8)

THE MIDNIGHT DELTA SERIES
Her Vigilant Seal (Book #1)

Her Loyal Seal (Book #2)

Her Adoring Seal (Book #3)

Sealed with a Kiss (Book #4)

Her Daring Seal (Book #5)

Her Fierce Seal (Book #6)

A Seals Vigilant Heart (Book #7)

Her Dominant Seal (Book #8)

Her Relentless Seal (Book #9)

Her Treasured Seal (Book #10)

Her Unbroken Seal (Book #11)

THE LONG ROAD HOME

Defending Home

Home Again

FATE HARBOR

Trusting Chance

Protecting Olivia

Isabella's Submission

Claiming Kara

Cherishing Brianna

SILVER SEALS

Seal At Sunrise

SHADOWS ALLIANCE SERIES

Declan

Made in the USA
Las Vegas, NV
28 March 2025